MW00386848

Tumbling Blocks

A Gabby Gordon Mystery

By

Edward F. Finch

Tumbling Blocks

Tumbling Blocks © 2015 by Edward F. Finch

This is a work of fiction. There is no conscious attempt to portray any actual person or character, living or dead. Any resemblance between any actual person, living or dead, and a character herein, is purely coincidental.

Any actual business, television program, motion picture, or product referenced in this work is done so without the knowledge or permission of the trademark or copyright holder. Their use herein does not imply authorization for said use.

All rights to this work are reserved under the copyright laws. Compliance with the copyright law means that this work, in whole or in part, may not be copied, scanned, reproduced or distributed in any form, electronic or otherwise, without the expressed written permission of the copyright holder.

Cover photograph by James E. Finch.

Tumbling Blocks

For

Sherbug, Me-Me-Kiss, & Tosh

The Parapet

R. Samuel Dooley's head droops so deeply that the two gals at the other end of the bar think he's resting it on his almost empty tumbler. The bar of O'Maddy's, situated on the ground floor of downtown Freeport's Hampton Inn, is empty but for Dooley's sagging pate and the two female bartenders.

"Does he actually really get like this hammered like I mean all the time?" queries Sandy, who is working her first night at the popular watering hole.

"Actually, he comes in here every night at seven, lays a twenty on the bar, gets a rum and Diet Coke. Then like every half hour or so he'll ask us to top it off, which we do but only with the Diet Coke. By seven thirty he's as smashed as he will get all night." Melody's response is accompanied by a slow shaking of her head.

"You've gotta be kiddin'? Like all he has is one shot of rum the entire freakin' night?"

"He'll stagger out of here when we tell him it's time to go. Then he'll drive home and repeat it all every night."

"Didn't this guy actually like teach Drivers Ed at the high school? I think I had him."

Melody's peace symbol earrings jingle as she nods her head. "The dude's like retired now, but, yeah, taught most of us to drive."

"Cops ever nail him for DUI?"

"They stopped trying. One shot of rum over a five hour period is not enough to fail a breathalyzer. And he manages to be a safe driver on his way home."

"Man, that's just whacko!"

"Dude's a sober drunk, what can I say? But he does tip well, what's left of the twenty each night goes to whoever's on the bar. Usually about ten bucks, depending on whether or not you charge him every time you top off his Diet Coke."

Tumbling Blocks

The Bud Light digital clock on the wall behind the bar has just ticked over to twelve midnight when the plate glass windows begin to rattle. The hum of the compressors in the coolers is drowned out by an increasingly loud rumble. At first the gals think all of the vibration is from two semi's rolling down Galena Avenue past the bar. But when glasses start falling off shelves they know it's something unusual. The tremor and roar feels like hundreds of box cars trundling by; the din echoing off the buildings of the downtown.

Heading to the north windows as the noise begins to subside, Melody and Sandy are in time to see a wall of water roiling toward them. The force of the tsunami – in this case about 250 tons of water – hits the side of the Hampton Inn-O'Maddy's with such force that all of the bar's windows are blown in, including the one where the girls are standing.

At the last second, both duck below the top of the counter that runs along the windows. As the tidal wave barges in, that counter and the equipment beneath it absorb most of the wave's impact. The force of the flood, however, pushes the counter across the three foot gap so that it comes to rest against the bar, pinning the women beneath the bar and the counter. Both units, however, remain upright, as does Dooley on his stool, though an eddy of water swirls around the legs of his bar stool even as all the other stools are carried away in the deluge.

Looking up from his glass as the sounds of rushing water wane, he slurs, "Ladies, ya got time to top this off before ya close?"

Chapter 1

G abby's cell rings, jarring her from a deep sleep. *That's not the right sound for the alarm* she thinks as she gropes for the source of the rude intrusion. "Yeah?"

"Gabriel Gordon?"

"Sorta."

"This is the Freeport Police. Do you own the building at 12 South Galena Avenue?"

"What? Who? What time is it?"

"Two twenty A.M. Miss Gordon, are you awake?"

"I'm gettin' there. Now what's this about?"

"Do you own the building at 12 South Galena Avenue?"

"Yes. I just bought it. We closed on it this afternoon. Is there a problem? Been a break-in?"

"No, Miss Gordon, no break-in. But there is a problem. Your building just fell down."

"What do you mean it 'just fell down'?"

"It collapsed into the street and then dumped tons of water down Galena. You better come down here."

"Anyone hurt?"

"A couple women working at O'Maddy's got some bruises and cuts, but nothing serious. You do need to come down here now. The Mayor, the Chief of Police, and the City Engineer all want to talk to you immediately."

"Do they want me to pick-up bricks at two-thirty in the morning?"

"I think that's the general idea. What's left of the building is blocking three lanes of Galena, which is a state highway. Gonna play hell with morning traffic."

"OK, I'll be there in a short while."

After she hangs up, Gabby stares at the wall across from her bed. *Is this somebody's idea of a joke?*

Thumbing her cell to "recent calls," she sees that the caller ID is indeed the Freeport Police Department. *Shit and shoved in it.*

Tumbling Blocks

Attorney by day, Gabriel Gordon rehabilitates old buildings as an avocation. The only child of a carpenter who wanted a son, she was stuck with the male spelling of her name and became the designated substitute son learning carpentry and building trades even as she was indoctrinated to bleed Cubby Blue, root for 'da Bears, and head to law school.

She hits the button for Glenn's number and waits for him to shake out of whatever dream he's having. When the unanswered call goes to voice mail, she redials. Just before it would have kicked over again a very groggy Glenn answers, "Gabby, what's goin' on?"

"Big problem. Our building just collapsed onto Galena Avenue."

"What? Say that again."

"It collapsed."

"What building?"

"The Bresch Building. You know the one we purchased about fourteen hours ago? Now it's blocking three lanes of Galena. I'm on my way there now. You probably ought to get down there, too."

"Geez Louise Gertrude! What the hell happened?"

"I've got no idea. I'll see you there in about an hour twenty."

"OK. I'm up and movin'."

Gabby hangs up, and begins to get dressed. At 5' 11" with shoulder length auburn hair and green eyes, she attracts more attention than she prefers from males who have yet to learn the rules defining unwanted advances. Once dressed, which takes all of three minutes, she dials Glenn again. And again he picks up on the last ring before going to voice mail.

"Yeah?"

"Building collapsed. Get your tush moving, Double N!" Gabby's pet name for her fiancé is "double N," based on the spelling of his first name.

"Gotch ya, coach. Wait, you mean I'm not having a nightmare about the building?"

6

Tumbling Blocks

"No, it's for real. Please get down there. Love ya."

"Love you, too. Oh, and honey, please don't do something stupid like climb on the debris. Can you do that for me?"

"I got it. No climbing on our $28,000 pile of bricks."

As she drives downtown, her mind races over the events of the past month as she and Glenn deliberated over the purchase of the Bresch Building. Glenn Logan, an architect specializing in historic restorations, currently works for a firm in Madison, Wisconsin, but plans to open his own business once they are married. While life might have been easier for them if they were living together, both agree that their prior marriages are reasons to be cautious about pushing their relationship too quickly in any direction, especially since they both have moral qualms about cohabitation.

They intended to renovate the Bresch Building into office space for Glenn and gain some income producing apartments on the top two floors. Now those plans lay in ruins.

Chapter 2

T he scene downtown is right out of a Hollywood disaster movie. Emergency vehicles everywhere: red, blue, white and yellow lights flashing and reflecting off the windows and sides of the surrounding buildings. City police, sheriff deputies, state police, EMTs, fire trucks, NiCor, ComEd, City Water and Sewer, telephone company, etc., etc., etc. Later Gabby will swear that she even saw a car from the Secretary of State's Police.

"Is this a convention for anyone with a flashing light?" Gabby grouches to the policeman who lets her through the cordon around the scene.

"Miss Gordon," intones Mayor Jackson. "Thanks for coming so quickly. We've no idea what caused this, but we need to get this cleared away as soon as possible. Do you have insurance?"

"Yes, it was supposed to go into effect at midnight. What time did this happen?"

"The two witnesses down at O'Maddy's said it was 12:01 A.M. Lucky you."

"We'll see about that, as I am sure some insurance company attorney will want to argue that one in court if they get stuck paying for this mess."

"There's a bit of irony for ya," throws in the Deputy Police Chief standing next to the Mayor. "Former law office collapse ends in law suit."

"And there's the problem," Police Chief Mason adds. "The insurance company adjustors are going to want to see this before any of it gets moved. That could take a couple days between them getting here and when we get construction crews cleaning the streets."

"Looks to me like the debris that is blocking the two lanes the furthest from the building will yield the least clues about what happened," Gabby responds. "I will do what I can to get them cleared within the next twelve hours, if that will help."

"That would be great," the Mayor says with relief. "At least we can have traffic moving in both directions. One lane each way would be better than having to detour all traffic."

A city worker, whom Gabby later learns is the City Engineer, walks up to the group and reports to the Mayor,

"NiCor says there are no gas leaks and ComEd says the electricity was off and none of the surrounding buildings were affected. The city water was already shut off since the building had been vacant for so many years."

"So, there is no immediate danger of explosion or electric shock?" Jackson asks.

"I think the site is as safe as it can be made until we have the debris cleared."

"Did the building have a basement?" the Mayor questions.

"Yes," Gabby interjects. "Had a dirt floor that sat a little over six feet below grade."

The City Engineer gives Gabby a strange look, as if to ask *how does this woman with a pony tail pulled through the back of a Cubs ball cap know what 'below grade' means?*

Jackson catches the look and quickly notes, "Attorney Gabriel Gordon, building's owner; this is City Engineer Keith Doris."

Keith nods to Gabby before heading towards two approaching Street Department workers.

Tumbling Blocks

Chapter 3

Gabby walks around the outer rim of the jumbled pile of bricks, plaster and splintered wood. Only the front half of the building has collapsed. The back half is still standing, but at a precarious angle.

It appears to her that the building has fallen at about a forty-five degree angle to the north-south street that runs in front of it. In Gabby's mind a worse alternative forms: *At least it did not fall straight across to the east, which would have not only blocked all four lanes of Galena, but would have damaged the Fifth/Third Bank parking deck across the street, too.*

Fortunately there is an alley and a small parking lot to the immediate south of the building which means that the next building appears to have little, if any damage. Also, there is a gap of almost a foot between the Bresch Building and the two-level parking garage to its north, so there is no apparent damage to that structure, either. Galena Avenue at the point where it passes in front of the now tumbled down building is on a steep angle going south toward the Hampton Inn.

If the building was going to collapse, this was probably the least damage it could do in the process, Gabby thinks as she surveys the shambles.

She is about to climb up the pile of rubble that lay across the alley when someone grabs her. "You promised not to go climbing on piles of rubble." It's Glenn.

Gabby smiles when she sees his face and black, wavy hair. "I know, but I figured this was a safe pile since it is on top of the alley, not over the basement."

In his early thirties he stands six feet tall with a well maintained body--wide shoulders and tight abs narrowing at the hips, sculpted muscles showing from his short-sleeved shirt all pointing to him working out on a regular basis.

"Promise is a promise, alley or no alley." Glenn looks around at the heap that had been the 126 year old building. "What a freakin' mess. Anyone hurt?"

10

Tumbling Blocks

"Couple waitresses at O''Maddy's got some cuts and bruises. That's all that's been reported."

"What took out the windows at the bar?"

"According to what I've been told it was a huge wall of water, like a tidal wave."

"Surely a broken water main half a block away wouldn't do that much damage?"

"Agreed. But the water to the building has been turned off for ten years or more. So where did it come from?"

"The roof?"

"The police said that the water not only broke the windows, it moved a counter over to the bar before partially flooding the basement of the hotel."

"That's one heck of a lot of water."

An insurance company's subsequent investigation determines that the roof of the building, which was flat but surrounded by a 2-foot high parapet, was full of water. The City Engineer calculated that the 40' X 100' building with a 2-foot parapet could have contained as much as 8,000 cubic feet of water.

"A gallon of water weighs about eight point three pounds, and eight thousand cubic feet of water would equal over fifty-five thousand gallons," Glenn later explains. "That comes to some two hundred forty-nine tons of water."

The manager of the Hampton Inn later informs investigators that a guest occupying the top corner room overlooking the area of the Bresch Building reported seeing what looked like a "swimming pool" on the roof the evening before the collapse. He also reported that he thought he saw a couple geese floating on the rooftop pond.

The insurance investigator's report noted, "At some point one of the two roof drains had been closed off by the previous owner because it leaked into the basement. The other drain probably became plugged with debris over the years. The heavy rains in the weeks before the collapse had turned the roof into a lake, as well as weakening the foundation. The top-heavy building only needed vibrations from a heavily loaded semi-trailer truck moving past to bring down the structure."

Chapter 4

B y one the next afternoon, two lanes of Galena are open, even as insurance investigators scramble over the crumbled remains. Gabby is just sitting down at the desk in her office, still wearing the faded blue jeans and indigo chambray shirt she'd hastily thrown on in the middle of the night. Glenn is collapsed into a chair in the corner and seems about to fall asleep when Gabby's cell rings.

"Hello."

"Miss Gordon, this is City Engineer Doris. I think you need to come back down here to see something."

"Is it urgent?"

"That I don't know, but I think you will find it very interesting."

Her curiosity piqued, Gabby rouses Glenn and they head on foot back to the site of their crumbled dreams.

When they arrive at the scene, Keith leads them up a path in the rubble along the north edge of the toppled building. When they are standing at about the level of the second floor, he points over to a concrete structure which stands partially exposed amid the debris.

"What the heck is that?" Gabby asks.

"Without looking at it closer, I'd say it's like a bank vault. Built within the building, but of stronger material."

"There was no vault when we toured the building," Gabby puzzles. "Glenn, do you remember anything like that?"

"No. No vault. But wait there was a bump-out on the first floor – about ten by ten. It had no door that I could find. I noticed a similar structure beneath it in the basement. The first floor walls had been plastered over and they matched the rest of the interior."

"You suppose the door to the vault, or whatever it is, was plastered over, too?"

"Who knows?"

13

Tumbling Blocks

On impulse, Gabby jumps the two foot gap from where she is standing to the top of the "vault."

"Hey!" Glenn yells. "No climbing on the debris."

"If this thing withstood the building going down, it'll hold me."

With that Gabby begins pushing bricks and chunks of plaster off the wood floor that remains atop part of the mystery structure.

"Check this out," she calls to Glenn as she motions to him.

Soon Gabby, Glenn and Keith are standing on the structure.

"Help me push this off. I think there's something under it."

All three grab the edge of what is left of the floor over the structure only to discover that what they are lifting is a trap door. Adjusting their holds, the three roll the section of floor over the side. The scrapping and creaking sounds of the movement of the floor section end in a loud crash, startling the gaggle of on-lookers standing behind barricades across the street. At Gabby's feet is the type of door found on a bank vault; only this one is built into the top of the structure.

"This is odd, very odd," Glenn comments wryly as they stare at the vault door on which they are standing.

As fate would have it, the uncovering of the safe's door is caught by a TV crew from Rockford. The cameraman and reporter are standing on the parking deck of Security First Title Company to the north where they have a clear view of the trio as they uncover the mysterious vault and its door. Rockford is a mere 25 miles from Freeport so TV stations from there cover events in Freeport as part of their local news.

Chapter 5

As Gabby walks into Higher Grounds the next morning for her daily latte, a slightly built man in a three piece suit approaches. She recognizes Amery Stocker, a local insurance agent and city council member.

"Mr. Stocker, good to see you," Gabby begins as a blender roars to life to create a frappe for some other customer.

"Miss Gordon, I heard that you frequent this place in the mornings, so I thought I'd try to catch you here rather than intrude on your work day."

"Well, what can I do for you?"

"Did you see the local news last night?"

"Don't watch much TV." Gabby responds in a half lie. In fact, she never watches TV, but finds that people assume she's lying if she so states. Hence her hedge in answering Stocker's query.

"I saw the news last night. As you may not know, my father, The Colonel, was a client of the Bresches and I have long believed that a journal or diary which The Colonel kept during the war was entrusted to the safe keeping of the Bresches. I imagine that it has no value beyond that of my family wanting to preserve a piece of the history my father helped make."

"I think I know where you're going, Mr. Stocker..."

"Please, call me Amery. Yes, if it is in that vault or whatever you've uncovered, we would very much appreciate its return. We have long assumed that the journal was lost along with all of the files of the Bresch law practice, so we are hopeful that it can now be recovered."

"There being no other indication of a reason for it being in the files, we will gladly return it to you and your family."

"Excellent. I appreciate your time. Have a good day."

"Thanks. You, too."

As Amery leaves, Gabby thinks to herself: *You'll not win friends intruding on my morning latte, mister. Better call my office for an appointment next time.*

Tumbling Blocks

The conversation with Stocker over, Gabby's cellphone begins to chirp. It's her office. When she answers, Gabby hears the distinctive voice of Emma Zangara, the officer manager. The office is getting flooded with phone calls for Gabby.

Grudgingly Gabby gets her latte to go and then is off to the offices of Weston and Sanderson. Having had her morning routine disrupted—an hour to sip her latte, read the *Chicago Tribune* and mentally prepare for the day—she now is slightly annoyed. *Why couldn't he just make an appointment like any other respectful person?*

Hired by Weston and Sanderson right out of law school, Gabby has spent seven years with the firm. This morning she doesn't even get to the door of her private office before she is handed a stack of phone messages all asking about the contents of the mystery vault. Amery's query is only the tip of the iceberg when it comes to the plethora of queries and suggestions that the TV coverage elicited about what might be inside. One caller left a message postulating that Jimmy Hoffa's body is in there.

Recalling few facts about the prior owners, Gabby calls her good friend Dr. H. Elmer Barnes, Executive Director of the Stephenson County Museum, to obtain a full history of the building.

"My dear, I figured you'd call at some point," Barnes begins with his slightly Harvard / East Coast accent. "We've had numerous calls from news media all over the map. Seems the television segment last night got picked up by other stations around the country, and has been posted on YouTube. Now everyone wants to know to whom the secret vault might have belonged. I have delayed responding so that I could get the information to you first, but it's not that big of a secret.

"I'll FAX the sheet to you, but suffice it to say for now that the building was built in 1888 by John B. Whiting, an attorney. Eventually he sold it to his junior partner Nicholas Israel Bresch. The building remained the law offices of the

16

Bresches through three generations, with Nicholas Israel Bresch, the third, being the last to occupy it."

"When did the number three Bresch close the business?"

"Oh, he didn't, my dear. Soon after Bresch, Jr. died in 1980, his son disappeared and was never heard from again."

"Was foul play involved?"

"That I do not know. Perhaps one of the senior partners from your firm might know more. The fraternity of the bar is as gossipy as any other profession, so if there is scandal there, one of them will probably know. I'll FAX over this sheet. It is from the Historic Buildings Commission report from a couple years ago. Let me know if there is anything else we can do."

Her curiosity piqued, Gabby walks across the firm's office suite to Kenneth Sanderson's office. One of the two senior partners of Weston and Sanderson, Kenneth is semi-retired, limiting his law practice to a few long-term clients. He is alone and his door is open so Gabby knocks.

"Tsk, yes, Gabby, come on in," Kenneth responds. The trim, gray haired attorney motions to a chair. "Tsk, with what may I help you?"

"Can you tell me anything about the Bresch law practice?"

"Tsk," is the sound with which he begins every statement. It is not the sound of disdain like "tsk-tsk," but the sound of pause before speaking, sort of a tongue to roof of mouth sound in place of the more commonly heard "aah." Sam does a hilarious imitation of him, so Gabby always has to stay focused when talking with Sanderson lest she gets caught being amused recalling Sam's rendition.

"Tsk, that's a rather delicate subject. The firm, going back to the senior Bresch, was one of the stalwarts of the legal profession in the county. He wrote the Will of the very wealthy Jeremiah Winfrey, and that Will became a target of some litigation I believe. To the best of my knowledge the elder

Tumbling Blocks

Bresch died in about 1966, which is when Hector Weston and I formed this firm.

"Tsk, Bresch, Jr., was as good a lawyer as his father and the firm continued to handle many of the county's wealthier clients. His son, Nicholas the third, whom most of us called 'Nick," was not quite the top notched attorney that his father and grandfather had been. However, he took over a healthy practice. Around 1980 or so Bresch, Jr., died and within ten months Nick disappeared along with his secretary. There was lots of speculation about what happened. The police investigated and eventually Elizabeth Bresch, Nick's abandoned wife, admitted that she had received a letter from her truant husband confessing to leaving her and heading to places unspecified. Nick's secretary was a Shiloh Deming, if I recall, and a very fetching young lady. Nick supposedly had emptied all the bank accounts before he fled—both the firm's and his personal accounts. According to Elizabeth all she was left with were a couple Certificates of Deposit, a mortgaged house and two children to rear.

"What happened to the files of the law practice?"

"Tsk, that was the hardest part of the incident to decipher. No one could find them. The building was searched several times, but nothing was uncovered. There was pending litigation on which Bresch was working, there were copies of Wills, Trusts and other documents which clients had entrusted to the Bresch firm, all vanished just like Nick and Shiloh."

"So it would seem that many of the calls I am getting are from people who have been waiting over thirty years for information contained in those files. They are all hoping that the files are in the vault which was revealed by the collapse of the building."

"Tsk, I think you are correct. This will take some sorting out, assuming the files are in that vault. You would be well advised to consult the professional standards set by the Illinois Supreme Court for handling the files of defunct law practices."

Tumbling Blocks

"Most certainly and thanks for the information. You might want to discuss with Hector how the firm will want me to handle all this if the files are indeed in the vault."

"Tsk, thanks for being considerate enough to bring Weston and Sanderson into your calculations."

Chapter 6

S am is waiting in Gabby's office when the interview with
Sanderson ends.
"So, what did Old 'Tsker' have to say?" asks Sam, the
only truly free thinker Gabby has ever met. She was hired at the
law firm because Gabby liked her unconventional thinking, and
her antics make life bearable and sometimes even fun in what is
a generally stuffy law practice. Apart from her propensity of
speaking very rapidly and peppering her speech with
scatological words and phrases, she is a highly competent legal
secretary. Sporting a large collection of body art, Sam is forced
by the firm's policies to wear long sleeved tops even on hot July
days.

"Sam, stop that. Someone might hear you."

"It's not like everyone in the office gets in on the
imitations and as for Old 'Tsker, I think it'd go right over his
head. So, when are ya gonna open the vault? Kinda like that
Geraldo Rivera thing with Al Capone's basement. 'What secrets
are hidden behind this wall?'"

"Probably none and I'll have a ton of phone calls to
return telling people what they don't want to hear."

"But if there are files in there, what are you going to do
with them?"

"That will be a mess. If they are there, then it would be
almost seventy years of accumulated legal practice files. Sorting
them and getting a handle on what's where will take a good deal
of time. We don't have room for them here, at least not while
they're being sorted; plus the staff time to do all the sorting. The
building collapsing is enough of a nightmare, but the legal
implications of long lost files are even bigger. Who gets what
and how to deal with any cases that remain open will be one big
headache.

"Sanderson said that the Bresch firm handled the estate
of some guy named Jeremiah Winfrey and that it generated

litigation. If there are folks who still have issues with that estate, then we could have some fun litigating it."

Chapter 7

G abby drops back into her chair and closes her eyes as she struggles to get some perspective on what has started out as a rather unusual day. When the phone on her desk rings, Sam picks up for Gabby.

"Miss Gordon's office. Oh, thanks Emma, I'll tell her." Laying the receiver back in its cradle, Sam announces, "You're nine o'clock appointment is here."

"Refresh my memory."

"Sisters named D'Ville. Said it had something to do with an insurance claim."

"When did they make the appointment?"

"Couple weeks ago."

"Good! Show them in. It'll be nice to think about something other than the Bresch Building for a few minutes."

Sam leaves but quickly returns with two women in tow. Both of whom are in their early thirties, both wearing miniskirts that are way too short given their overweight conditions, and both having puffed up hairdos that went out of style in the '90s. Gum smacking and jangling bracelets completed their first and enduring impression.

"Hello, welcome to Weston and Sanderson," Gabby begins as she holds out her hand.

"Hey, I'm Rita and this is my twin sister Marga."

"Pleased to meet ya," Marga says following it with a loud pop of her gum.

"Please have a seat at the table over here and then tell me what I can do for you."

"Well (pop, smack), we gotta a problem with an insurance company," Rita begins in a chatty style.

"Yeah, the bastards won't pay up on our double wide burning up."

"Yeah, we lost everythin'. All that Mama and Papa left us was in that double wide."

Tumbling Blocks

"Normally, I do not handle this type of case. I specialize in Wills and Estates. But we do have an attorney here who could look at your case."

"Yeah, well (smack, pop), we heard all about you handling that scummy lawyer from Chicago, so we figure you're the kind 'torney we need, seein' we're dealin' wit' insurance 'torneys. They probably share their jeans with dem Chicago 'torneys," Rita counters.

"Yeah, heard about that Chicago 'torney dying in your house when he had a gun and all."

"But he slipped and fell to his death. I had nothing to do with it. I did not even see it happen."

"Well, our man Brad on the radio doin' the news made it sound like you got the guy. Don't ya just love that man's voice? Makes ya wanna cuddle up with him. Brad, Brad, Brad."

"Yeah, sure does. And that Andy Canon guy on the early morning TV from Rockford. Deep down rumbles when he talks. We gets up early just to listen to him. Yummmm!"

"Yes, but let's get back to your house burning down."

"See, all we had was that double wide out on Henderson Road. Rita and me not bein' too good with money and jobs, but Papa figured we'd always have a place to live when he and Mama was gone, God rest 'em, so they left it to us. But now it's burned to the ground and we got nothin'. Been livin' out at the old Holiday Inn, but that's getting' old."

"Insurance company says that the fire that burned up all Mama and Papa left us was not covered by our policy. Fire's a fire if ya ask me."

"How did the fire start?"

" 'Tility power pole transformer 'sploded."

"Well, that should be the electric company's fault."

"Well, it weren't the 'splosion started the fire in the double wide, but the hawk."

"Hawk?"

"Yep! Poor dumb assed bird sittin' on that transformer mindin' his own business."

"Zap! Quicker an' ya can say 'fried chicken,' that bird is on fire and falls in the dry grass along the road deader 'an a door nail."

"The burnin' bird sets the grass a fir and before we knew what was happin' the fir's gots hold of our double wide."

"Yep, the very double wide Mama and Papa left us for scurity."

"Insurance company says it's the 'lectric company's problem."

"Power company says it were an act of God or Mother Nuture or some such shit."

"We think they're in cahoots."

"In what?"

"That's what Papa used to call it when a couple folks with lots of money tries to cheat little folks like us. Cahoots."

"This is an interesting case. Will you excuse me a minute? I'll be right back."

Gabby goes down the hall to the office of Kallen Moorsman, another associate at the firm. Soon Gabby returns with Kallen in tow.

"Ladies, I'd like you to meet Kallen Moorsman, an attorney who specializes in cases involving insurance companies. Kallen, this is Rita, no Marga and Rita D'Ville."

"Pleased to me ya (pop!)," Rita says as she shakes Kallen's hand.

"Case you're wondering 'bout our names, Rita and me was conceived after a Jimmy Buffet concert in the back of Papa's 1960 Corvair."

"That's where Mama and Papa met, and Papa always said it was the smoothest ride he ever had."

"That's how we got our names. Not many folks can say that."

"I agree," says Kallen while raising her eyebrows and repressing a smile. Turning to Gabby she asks, "And why am I here?"

"Do your 'Regan-from-the-Exorcist' imitation for the D'Ville sisters," Gabby responds.

"What?"

"Just do it, humor me."

Shrugging her shoulders, Kallen says in a very deep, gravelly voice, "Mama."

"Uhhhh! That sent slivers down my spine," Marga moans.

"Any woman 'torney sound like that gotta be OK. We'll work with her."

"Why don't you ladies head down to my conference room and I'll take some notes about your problem." Led by Rita, the two file out of Gabby's office. Kallen rolls her eyes and turns to Gabby as she whispers, "I will get you for this."

Chapter 8

No sooner had Gabby sat back down after getting the D'Ville twins out of her office then her phone rings again. It was Sam: "A lady named Betty Bresch is here to see you. She doesn't have an appointment, but she is most insistent on seeing you now. I'd say she is being rude to the point of obnoxious on the subject. Shall I get rid of her?"

"No, I figured she'd show up sooner or later. This day has gone from an annoyance to plain weird and who knows where this conversation is going to go. I'll come out to the lobby and escort her back."

Curiously, Gabby has never met Mrs. Bresch, even though they transacted the sale of the Bresch building the day before. Mrs. Bresch acted through her attorney and did not attend the closing on the property.

Elizabeth Bresch, generally called Betty to her face by people who know her, is obviously impatient as she stands in the middle of the waiting area. The wide variety of chairs and couches do not attract her. At 5' 2", the slightly graying brunette is well into a middle age spread that is not hidden by her expensive slacks and top.

"You must be Mrs. Bresch. I'm Gabriel Gordon."

"I know who you are. Saw you on TV last night. Call me Elizabeth or Betty, but not 'Mrs. anything'."

"I see. Why don't you come back to my office?"

Gabby no sooner closes the door to her office then Betty starts, "I want everything in that vault thing turned over to me as soon as you have it open."

"Ms. Bresch, please have a seat."

"There'll be no need. Just deliver to me whatever you find in that safe."

"Perhaps you do not understand the legal rights which you ceded to me and Glenn Logan when you signed over the deed yesterday. Any and all contents of the building belong to us now. Besides, professional standards dictate that any legal documents belong to the clients for whom they were created. Only the work done by the attorney, like notes and drafts, belong to the attorney. You made no stipulations in the sales contract about anything inside the building to which you lay claim, especially any legal work which your husband may have created."

"Well, this is all bullshit. I've had enough jerking around from lawyers over the past thirty years. Anything in that safe is from Nick's law practice and that of his father and grandfather. If there is any money to be made on it, it's mine, MINE! I'm the one who suffered the indignation of having a husband run off with a hippy flower child who couldn't type her way out of high school.

"The bastard I married left me with two kids to raise and no money. It took over seven years to have him declared legally dead so that I could get his life insurance and the money from his father's estate, which was in probate all that time."

She begins pacing around the office, spittle coming to her lips as she rattles off all her grievances like a telemarketer sprinting through a script.

"There I was with two kids in grade school and the whole town mocking 'poor Betty' who couldn't keep her husband. I was stuck with that big house on Stephenson Street, a huge mortgage and that wimpy dip shit emptied our bank accounts, as well as the accounts of the law practice before he ran out.

"Then the police came snooping around as if I killed him. Believe me, if I could have gotten my hands on that no good scum bag, he'd have been praying for death before I was done with him. And double for that slut Shiloh who was always so nice and condescending to me."

Betty is in a zone, neither looking at Gabby nor caring if Gabby is listening. The saga of her ordeal is all she can focus on once she gets going, and from the manner of its delivery, Gabby realizes that she has practiced this speech on a regular basis.

Tumbling Blocks

"I had to claw my way past his parents and their social crowd to get him to marry me. They did everything they could to keep us apart. I grew up on East Shawnee Street, but the snobs on West Stephenson Street thought that Nicholas I. Bresch, the Third, was too good for the likes of an Eastside bitch. But every time he came home from college or law school, it was to my house he headed, not to his parents'.

"But I finally got him. The weekend he came home after graduating from law school, we had our own private graduation party and before his parents could do anything I was pregnant and that was that. Those nose-in-the-air West Siders had no choice but to accept me; I was carrying the next generation of the Bresch dynasty."

Betty's voice rose in volume as she charged on, "And what did I get for all my effort? The bastard waits till his father dies and then runs off with a bitch with even less learnin' than me."

Now turning on Gabby, index finger wagging, Betty concludes, "SOOO, Miss high and mighty lawyer, all that there is mine. MINE, you hear me? I'll fight you until they lay me in my grave if you try to keep any of it."

"Ms Bresch, I do not pretend to know what you've been through. You have my sincere sympathy for the way life has treated you. But the fact remains that the deed you signed turning ownership of the building over to us is quite clear. You have no title to any of it."

"And you probably think you're gonna make money off those files! Money that rightfully ought to be mine."

Her temper beginning to rise, Gabby stands and glares across the desk at Betty, "If there is any money to be made off whatever is in that vault, it will probably not come close to the cost of having the remains of the building torn down and all of the debris hauled away."

"I don't give a shit, missy. What's mine is mine and I will get it one way or the other."

28

Tumbling Blocks

Later Gabby will regret that this woman goaded her into a shouting match, but Gabby's voice now rises in volume as her high school debater instincts take over: "Let me make five things perfectly clear: one, you are the one who failed to discover the vault, so the loss is on you; two, the deed you signed is clear and specific—any contents left in the building belong to the buyer; three, if we hadn't bought the building when we did, the tens of thousands of dollars this clean-up is costing would be on you since you didn't even have it insured; four, I've got more money than you, so if you want to fight this out in court, bring it on lady. All you'll be doing is wasting what little money you have; and five, just because you didn't know enough about your husband's business to know that there even was a vault and where it was located is on your head. Maybe if you were a little more involved in his life he wouldn't have run off with someone else."

Betty stands there shaking with anger, her lips moving with no sounds audible At length she snarls in a whisper, "You're a liar," as if that phrase is the penultimate condemnation.

"Now, can you find your way out or should I have Miss Greer show you?"

"You haven't heard the last of me you impertinent little bitch. And don't think that your spat with those Chicago hoods is going to intimidate me. I can find people with guns, too, you know."

Gabby is about to come out from behind her desk when Sam opens the door. "This way, Mrs. Bresch," Sam says with a polite smile that belies the ready fist behind her back.

Breathing through her teeth and stomping loudly on the hardwood floors, Betty Bresch marches toward the front door of Weston and Sanderson making so much noise that those employees who have not yet come out of the cubicles and offices at the sounds of the shouting do so now.

Tumbling Blocks

As she reaches the door, she turns to yell back at Gabby, "Yeah, I'm a bitch and if you don't believe me I can provide references!"

As soon as the front door closes behind Bresch, Sam closes Gabby's door and gives the trembling attorney a hug.

"Oh, my God," Gabby sighs. "I have never had anyone make me that angry. Not even my ex-husband Tom. Talk about somebody who knows how to push buttons."
Gabby slumps back in her chair, her arms hanging down at her side. "I suppose everyone in the office heard all of that?"

"No, only the last parts where both of you got so loud Emma turned up the radio on her desk to try to cover." Miss Emma Zangara is the office manager and she works very hard to maintain a high level of decorum at Weston and Sanderson. Sam's irreverent behavior is a constant burr under Emma's saddle.

"Are there other clients in the office?"

"No. Only us voles in the cubicles and a couple of the junior associates overheard the clash of the Titans. 'Tsker left for lunch just after Bitter Betty arrived."

"Bitter Betty?"

"According to the office grape vine, that's what most of Freeport calls her—behind her back of course. But she is one sour puss. When her son and daughter left for college they never came back, again according to hearsay in the cubicles. Her children never visit her and she has never been invited to their homes. Supposedly she has two grandkids she's never seen."

"That's sad, really sad. Must be some deep seated problems that would turn a person so acerbic her own children have completely shunned her."

"I suspect that she was always that way, but to a lesser extent before Nick left, and that's probably why he left. Gotta wonder what got 'em together in the first place."

Tumbling Blocks

"If you didn't catch it during the shouting match, he got her pregnant and then married her. Reading between the lines, I would bet that she got pregnant on purpose."

"You'll have to watch your back when it comes to this one."

"I've had a target on it before."

Chapter 9

B y the end of the week the calls about the Bresch files slow to a crawl and Gabby is beginning to think life might regain some normalcy. Sam is fielding the calls with a standard response, while taking the callers' contact information to facilitate future communications.

On Wednesday morning as Gabby arrives at her office she spends time reviewing her files on the Galway (aka Fallon) estate. Though it has been almost two years since the incidents that led to Galway's murder and the subsequent confrontation with Sean M. Scurry III, the gun toting attorney from Chicago, the issues of the estate of Galway/Fallon have yet to be resolved. Today at 11 AM she is to meet with representatives from Scurry's law firm—Malloy, Doran, Boylan and Hoban—to discuss the final settlement.

While Gabby is the principal heir to the multi-million dollar estate, there are legal questions about the original sources of the funds (Galway was a hitman for organized crime), but Scurry had been skimming hundreds of thousands of dollars from the account, so there is also the issue as to the firm's repayment of the principal plus interest and damages.

Five men in very expensive suits enter the offices of Weston and Sanderson for the meeting promptly at 11. Four of the men are from Malloy, et al., and the fifth is from the office of the United States Attorney for the District of Northern Illinois. Gabby has Madelyn Verde, now with Weston and Sanderson, as her legal counsel for the meeting.

As the meeting begins in the largest conference room of Weston and Sanderson, an elderly attorney who introduces himself as Sean Michael Hoban rises and faces Gabby.

"Miss Gordon, my grandson, Sean Scurry, is the person responsible for this whole mess. Both personally and professionally I am sickened by his deeds and can offer no excuse or explanation for his actions. His father died when Sean was a teen and I fear that he never matured beyond the emotional and ethical levels he had achieved when he suffered that loss.

"Trust me when I say that I am sincerely sorry for what he did and that our law firm was not diligent enough to safeguard the funds that were entrusted to our care by Mr. Fallon." At this point the man is overcome with remorse and grief, his trembling voice trailing into silence as he slumps back into his chair.

It seems obvious to Gabby that the other attorneys from Malloy, et al., are uncomfortable with the total admission their colleague has just made. Fortunately for them, Gabby has no plans to pursue further legal remedies in the case.

"We are prepared to offer you a settlement of two point three million dollars," begins an attorney who identified himself as Patrick Williams, an associate of the firm. As he hands Gabby a check, Daniel Creegan from the United States Attorney's office interrupts, "However, Miss Gordon, since the FBI has determined that the funds in the account were from criminal activities, we are confiscating the settlement." With that he takes the check and puts it in his fine grain leather folder.

"That amount," Williams continues, "was agreed upon by our firm and the U.S. Attorney's office. In addition, we are prepared to offer you a one million dollar settlement for your pain and suffering, which is independent of the funds in Mr. Fallon's Credit Suisse account. That is not subject to seizure by the Feds."

"Correct, but it comes with tax liabilities," adds Creegan.

"Doesn't everything," Gabby retorts.

"We have yet to make a final determination on the status of the twelve million dollars left to you in Fallon's USB account," Creegan continues.

All that is left is for Gabby to sign settlement papers drawn up by Malloy, et al., which Verde reviewed several weeks prior.

As they stand to leave, Hoban comes around the table and takes Gabby's hands. "I know we could have settled all this with FAXs and Emails, but I so wanted to express to you in person my sincere shame and humiliation over what happened. What my grandson did is not what the law firm of Malloy, Doran, Boylan and Hoban stands for or how we practice law. I hope you can find it in yourself to forgive us for what you went through."

"Mr. Hoban, I hold neither animosity nor rancor toward you or your firm. Events which can drive people into wrong decisions do not respect family ties, education levels or religious affiliations."

"You are very kind," Hoban responds as he gently guides Gabby away from the door as everyone else exits. When the room is empty save for the two of them, he whispers, "Don't let up on the Feds. They cannot prove anything about the USB account, as it was all money which Fallon's wife inherited from her father. Sooner or later you'll get all of it."

As Gabby walks past Sam's desk, she lays the one million dollar check down telling her secretary, "Please deposit this in my personal account and then cut a check for half the amount. Make it out to Community Care Haven. Send it with a letter noting that it is their share of the estate of John Galway. Madelyn will sort out the tax liability and let you know how much I need to forward to the IRS as withholding from the total amount."

Chapter 10

It took the better part of two weeks for the construction company to tear down the rest of the Bresch Building and haul away all the rubble. That only happened after the insurance adjusters spent more than a week crawling over the debris pile. In the end all that was left standing at 12 South Galena Avenue was a concrete monolith that was six feet below grade and ten feet above.

A very large white plastic tarp was placed over the vault since Gabby wasn't sure if the door in what was now the roof was water proof. A smaller, padded blue tarp was then added to make it harder for curiosity seekers to gain access to the top of the tower. Soon the wags around town were calling the blue and white structure "Gabby Smurf."

Any hopes Gabby had of opening the vault with any degree of privacy had no basis in reality. No sooner had the debris been cleared and "Gabby Smurf" stood alone in a now vacant lot then word spread that a pool had started on whether or not the Bresch files were inside. Odds were running two to one that the vault was empty. There was also a pool on whether or not Nick Bresch and his secretary's bodies would be found inside.

Efforts by several combination lock experts were unsuccessful at working the tumblers into proper alignment to open the steel door. All of them agreed that the fact that the door was lying on its back and that it had not been opened in over thirty years mitigated against any traditional method of finding the combination by listening as the tumblers aligned. In the end, Gabby and Glenn resorted to securing the services of a company which operate a very expensive thermal lance cutting torch.

"That torch generates over seven thousand degrees of heat, so it will punch through the vault door easily," Glenn explained. "It costs more per hour, but it will get the safe open quicker than any other form of acetylene and oxygen torch, so it will be cheaper in the long run."

Tumbling Blocks

Twenty-one days after the Bresch building collapsed workmen arrive to set up a crane to lift open the vault door. Even before the cutting torch is lit a large crowd gathers, mostly on the top level of the surrounding parking decks. Just on the outside chance that there are human remains in the vault, the county corner and sheriff are also on site.

"How the hell did they get that thing open back in the day?" is the most frequently asked question at the various restaurants and espresso bars where the town's brain trusts gather each morning.

Gabby was told by the workers who cleared the debris that they found a set of ropes and pulleys amid the rubble, so she assumes that the Bresches had some sort of system to swing the heavy steel door up from its' closed position.

"God help the person who was inside if the door closed by accident. I'm not sure even a very strong man could push the door up from the inside, at least far enough to get out," Glenn offers as he and Gabby watch the workers weld lifting hooks to the door.

The two men working the thermal lance cutting torch take almost an hour to cut out around the outer edge of the door, separating it from the steel bars that lock it.
With the crane already hooked to the door, the "grand reveal" comes as shadows of the late afternoon sun of a mid-June day are already creeping across the now naked "Gabby Smurf."

After the vault door is lifted aside, Gabby and Glenn climb a ladder to the top of the vault. Clicking on flashlights, they carefully scan the darkness below and then signal to the crew foreman to swing the door back into place.

Once on the ground, several members of both the local and national news media crowd around Gabby—the original coverage of the discovery of the mystery vault having generated interest outside of northwest Illinois.

"What did you see?"

"Could you see any bodies?"

"Are there files inside?"

36

Tumbling Blocks

"Is it where Nick Bresch and his secretary got trapped?"

"People. Please. I have a simple statement. We will pass out copies of the text after I've finished. I will not take questions at this time."

Removing a half-sheet of paper from her pocket, Gabby reads, "The contents of the vault appear to be only files. Until we have a chance to remove them to a secure location and examine them, we will not speculate as to their content. We did not see any human remains. We will provide more details when they become available."

Sam walks among the news people handing out copies of Gabby's statement as Glenn and Gabby head off toward Gabby's Wrangler. Gabby takes the three other versions of her statement out of other pockets and folds all of them together for disposal later. Not knowing what they'd find, she prepared four statements, each covering one of the most likely scenarios.

Chapter 11

O nce back at Babcook Manor, Gabby's French Norman style home, Glenn gets to work making dinner while Gabby sets the table and opens a couple bottles of wine. Glenn had previously prepared beef bourguignon and placed it in the oven before they left to go to the "grand reveal." He is just taking it from the oven when Sam in her rusty '95 Civic pulls on to the grounds. She is soon followed by Barnes in his '67 Triumph 4A roadster—British racing green, of course.

A dinner with Sam and Barnes is a weekly ritual for Gabby and Glenn. Needing reassurance from close friends after the killings in Babcook Manor two years before, these weekly dinners offer all four a chance to keep in close contact with the people who shared in that traumatic set of events.

Tonight Gabby and Glenn have asked Alys Mendenhall and Sarah Fuller to join the gathering for the first time. Life partners, Alys and Sarah had only a month before moved into the newly remodeled apartment above Babcook Manor's three car garage. Alys, a 6' 1" former collegiate long jumper, has short, black hair and a relaxed manner that belies a body tensed like a steel coil. She is a jack-of-all-trades who now maintains the grounds of the manor in lieu of their paying rent. Sarah is 5' 10", has shoulder length honey brown hair she keeps mostly in a pony-tail, as well as the physique of a long distance runner, which was her sport in both high school and college. She's a Physician's Assistant at FHN. The two also bring to the group Irish Red, Alys' four year old Irish Setter.

"How did you come up with his name?" Sam asks as she sits on the floor face-to-face with the friendly dog, rubbing her ears.

"Growing up I fell in love with Irish Setters after reading a couple novels about them," Alys answers.

"Ah, yes. 'Big Red' and 'Irish Red' by Jim Kjelgaard," Barnes jumps in. "I too read those novels in my youth."

Tumbling Blocks

"And thank you, Dr. Barnes," Alys says as she bows in Barnes' direction. "All these years I wondered how to pronounce his last name."

"Delighted to be of service, and please just call me Barnes; everyone else does," Barnes bows back.
It turns out that Irish Red is almost overly affectionate. Since arriving at Babcook, he's thrived in the open spaces of the manor's five fenced-in acres and Alys' almost obsessive grooming regimen.

The six have just settled into chairs around the dining room table when Gabby's cell rings.

"Excuse me for taking this. It's the contractor. Hello. Yes. Yes. OK. Yes. Thank you."
Five sets of expectant eyes silently query Gabby as she sits her cell phone on the table.

"They got the vault door back in place and then replaced the tarps. The overnight security guard we hired is there and they'll be ready in the morning to re-open."

"I confirmed with the temps on being available tomorrow at nine to begin sorting the files," Sam adds.

"It'll cost more per hour to have the crane lift out the file cabinets, but it will take less total time than hiring workmen to move individual files into boxes and then carry them up the ladder," Glenn, the self-proclaimed efficiency expert, explains to Barnes.

"Well, I for one will be most anxious to examine the files. I appreciate that they are to be considered confidential legal papers, but imagine the history there: the complete legal work of two full generations of a law firm. Could be most fascinating," Barnes seems to glow in anticipation at the trove about to be uncovered.

"We want you there as we begin to examine what comes out and I am confident that you'll respect the legal requirements," Gabby nods.

"Be assured that my lips will remain sealed. Except, of course, for this most excellent Bordeaux. My compliments to the sommelier." With that Barnes lightly touches his glass to Sam's before lifting it toward the others.

As they begin eating, Sarah compliments Gabby on the salad dressing. Gabby quickly admits that Glenn made the dressing, as well as the rest of the meal.

"Where did you learn to cook?" Sarah asks.

"Four years in college and two in grad school all spent working weekends at Lagniappe Brasserie, one of the Milwaukee area's premier French restaurants. I started out as a busboy, but when things were slow I'd ask the various chefs about what they did. Soon I was working on the salad line and making the dressings. Because I was always available to work weekends, the *Sous Chef* scheduled me as often as possible. Eventually I got so I could do all of the jobs in the kitchen and was working as the weekend station chef for seafood when I left after graduation."

"That's known as the *chef de partie*," Barnes informs the rest of the diners.

"They offered me the *Sous Chef* position just before I finished my master's degree, but I was intent on architecture as a career."

"Gabby, if you ever get tired of this guy's cooking, he can like dress my salad anytime," Sam says with a wink.

"Don't plan on that in the next fifty to sixty years," Gabby laughs as she touches her wine glass to Glenn's.

Chapter 12

L ater their conversation gets around to the status of the money Gabby had inherited. For the benefit of Sarah and Alys, Gabby elaborates on the circumstances.

"The whole matter was reviewed by the FBI and the U. S. Attorney's office. The Chicago law firm whose employees stole the money have made restitution, but the Feds consider all the money in the account as fruits of illegal activities, so they confiscated the settlement. But it looks like the second account may not be subject to confiscation since it was from Galway's wife's inheritance."

"Never mind that her father was the head of an organized crime syndicate and that his money undoubtedly also came from illicit sources," Glenn adds.

"What are you guys talking about? Who was this Galway?" Alys asks.

"Oh, much too long a story for tonight," Barnes intones as he looks over the top of his eyeglasses at Gabby. "Suffice it to say that he was once a resident of this magnificent hovel, worked as an assassin for organized crime, and put Gabby and Glenn through Hell before he himself was murdered."

The conversation pauses and everyone turns to watch Gabby as she mindlessly rolls wine around inside her glass, a rainbow of colors cascading down its sides. She is deep in thought as her mind flashes back to that terrible night when she and Glenn were trapped in the basement of the house with a killer looking for them. As her mind returns to the present she begins talking as if she's thinking aloud, "Now all we have to do is navigate the inheritance laws of Switzerland, and then the ones here if we decide to bring the money into the country."

"Might be simpler to move to Switzerland, but our hearts are stuck in the American Midwest," Glenn concludes.

"Guys, you'd actually give up a chance to live in like Switzerland?" Sam blurts.

Tumbling Blocks

"In truth," Barnes intones, "they could live anywhere in the European Union as the inheritance laws are now standardized there. Perhaps Provence or Bordeaux?" With that he again holds up his glass. "Buy your own vineyard, perhaps."

"Yeah, like the movie with Russell Crowe. What was that?" Sam asks while snapping her fingers trying to recall the title.

"*A Good Year*," Sarah offers. "One of my favorite movies."

In spite of the ribbing about living in Europe, Sam and Barnes are too polite to ask the burning question: "How much?" Another long pause in the conversation makes Gabby realize what is on everyone's mind.

"The account has a little over twelve million in it."

"Euros or dollars?" Barnes asks softly.

"Dollars," Gabby replies.

"Well, hell," Sam smiles, "let's toast to the nut job that put you through Hell, but at least rewarded you for like the actual trouble."

Sensing that there is a need to change the topic of conversation, Barnes asks, "Gabby, have you two decided what you're going to do with what will soon be a vacant lot?"

"No, we've not really discussed it. I imagine that it will cost us a good deal to have the vault removed once we've emptied it. There seems to be no way to come even close to recouping what we'll have spent just to get an empty lot."

"What about the insurance money?" Sarah queries.

"The reality is that the damages to the Hampton Inn and O'Maddy's will eat up a great deal of the policy's maximum coverage. Clearing away the debris, especially the rush job to get Galena cleared in the first twenty-four hours, will probably exceed the monetary limits of the policy. The rest will be on us, especially the cost of taking out the tower vault."

"I've not had time to test the structure under the cement, but I figure it will be heavily reinforced with steel rods, which will make destroying it very costly," Glenn opines.

Tumbling Blocks

"If I might be so bold as to make a suggestion," Barnes says with a twinkle in his eye, a sure foretelling of his offering something in jest. "One famous person who once visited our fair city was the Abolitionist and orator Frederick Douglass, who was probably the most well-known Black American of his day. It was in 1856 when he came. We have nothing which commemorates that great man's speech here. He spoke at a public gathering in the original county courthouse. That building was in deplorable condition when he spoke and he remarked on that fact.

"My suggestion would be to make the vacant lot into a small park, leave the tower vault in place and locate a statue of Frederick Douglass on top. The Douglass image could be posed pointing at the current courthouse and bear an inscription of what Douglass said that night in Freeport."

"What did he say?" Sam asks, completely believing that Barnes' plan is serious.

"Speaking of the courthouse, he said, 'of all the Godforsaken places, this beats them all.' I think that would be very apropos considering the hideous nature of the architecture of the present courthouse."

As conversation drifts off into other topics and they migrate into the family room, Gabby's thoughts are often distracted with the details of the following day's work. However, Glenn becomes aware of the way Sam keeps looking at Barnes—a mixture of awe and admiration bordering on puppy love. Barnes is his usual loquacious and gracious self, ever the best guest and conversationalist. If he notices Sam's rapt attention to his every word, he does not show it.

After their guests leave and Glenn is putting away the last of the clean dishes, Gabby comes up behind him, wraps her arms around his waist and lays her head on his back.

"Thanks for the great meal and for being so steady through all this. Seems like all I ever do is get you in the middle of my troubles."

"*Au contraire*, my dear. Buying that building was my idea, and I couldn't think of another person with whom I prefer to be in trouble."

As she slightly loosens her hug Glenn turns within her encircling arms to face her.

"Heading home soon?" she asks.

"Yeah. I'll need to be on the road early tomorrow to be here when they begin pulling out the files."

"I forgot to ask this morning, any word from the Tribunal?"

"No. Maybe something came today. Do these things always take this long?"

"I have no idea. Mine went quickly and I don't see why yours is taking so long. It is a simpler case than mine. But, every annulment is different."

"Hard to set a date when we're stuck in limbo over my annulment. By the way, you catch that? I actually used the word 'limbo'."

"And correctly, too. See all those hours of religious instruction are paying off."

"Well, do you want me to call you when I get back to my place?"

"Sure. I won't sleep much tonight, so I doubt you'll wake me."

"By the way, did you happen to see the way Sam was looking at Barnes tonight?"

"No, why?"

"I'd say somebody is infatuated with the good doctor."

"Sam? Really? I can't imagine that. Must be your imagination. You sure you're OK to drive. Not too much wine?"

"Two glasses in three and a half hours. I'm sure I'm OK and no, it was not the wine that caused me to read things into Sam and Doc."

Gabby is still staring at the ceiling over her bed when Glenn calls to say that there was a letter which informed him that his request for an annulment of his marriage to Alexi is being placed on hold pending further investigation and testimony. They agree to let the disconcerting news rest while they sort out the contents of the tower vault. Both fear, but are reluctant to say it to each other, that they are about to open the proverbial Pandora's Box when it comes to the vault.

Chapter 13

There is no Chapter 13.

Chapter 14

E ngaging in a process none of them had ever seen before,
the removal of the files still proceeds much more
smoothly than Gabby had first hoped. By mid-afternoon
the vault is empty and much to the disappointment of the
gathered media and crowd of gawkers, no human remains are
discovered.

The two level vault—first floor and basement—contain
twelve legal-size file cabinets, most of them made of wood.
There is one fire-proof file cabinet, which is locked and
eventually requires a locksmith to open.

"Odd, very odd indeed," Glenn remarks looking at it
once it is on the ground. "Why put a fire-proof file cabinet
inside a fire-proof safe? Had to have taken six men and a horse
to move it to the second floor of the building and then lower it
down there to begin with."

"Perhaps its contents will reveal some long kept secrets
about some of Freeport's notable families," Barnes speculates
with glee.

Gabby rented the empty store front of the long defunct
Freeport Hardware to use as interim storage for the files.
Making a play on the fact that old files are sometimes stored in a
place called a repository and that in this instance they were
being sorted in a place that once sold metal files or rasps, Barnes
dubs the place the "Raspitory." The name catches on with
Gabby and her crew; soon they are all calling it the Raspitory

Four temp workers under Sam's supervision begin
indexing the contents of all the file cabinets as they are brought
into the make-shift work space. At Sam's insistence, all the data
is entered into Excel files that are backed up on two separate
flash drives as well as being saved on the three PCs purchased
for the project. One flash drive is stored in Weston and
Sanderson's vault at night while the other goes home with Sam.
All of this precaution is due to Sam's obsession with making

backups of computer files. She routinely makes backups of her backups.

Not wanting to expend the money to have an electronic security system installed for what is simply a temporary office now dubbed Raspitory, Gabby settles on a hired over-night security guard.

Just past 1:00 a.m. on the first night the files are out of the vault someone tries to break into the Raspitory. Attune to the situation in general, the Freeport Police Department increased patrols in that area of the downtown. As a roving patrol car turns down the alley behind the Raspitory, someone flees from the alcove which shelters it's backdoor. The would be intruder had yet to make enough noise to arouse the security guard inside when the approaching police car forced the unidentified individual to flee. Searches of the surrounding areas do not produce a suspect, leaving the police to speculate that whoever it was had access to another building in the immediate area. A copy of the report on the incident is eventually given to Gabby.

The locksmith opens the fire-proof safe the next day, though Gabby is back at Weston and Sanderson and Glenn is back at work in Madison by then. Soon Barnes and Sam are digging through some very old files, and it is Sam who makes the first interesting discovery—the hand-written war diary by Amery M. Stocker.

Generally called "The Colonel," Stocker was a widely known and likable man who worked at MICRO SWITCH / Honeywell after a career in the U.S. Army. His son is now a successful insurance agent and sits on the Freeport City Council. It was the younger Stocker who interrupted Gabby's morning routine in asking for the diary.

Sam shows it to Barnes, who immediately recognizes it as Stocker's World War II diary.

"As a rule, all those serving in the U.S. military during the war were enjoined from keeping such journals lest they fall into enemy hands and reveal secret information. That did not discourage many from keeping records of where and when they were involved in the war. Fascinating reading for historians and sometimes of great interest to the men's families," Barnes concludes.

"Why do you suppose Stocker gave it to his attorney?"

"Perhaps he just wanted it kept in a safe place, but he could just as easily have rented a safe deposit box at one of the local banks. There might be a clue about why his attorney was holding it if we knew what else was in its' folder."

Looking at the remaining contents of the folder, Sam relates, "The file appears to actually deal with a piece of artwork which Stocker donated to the Freeport Art Museum. Holy shit, and then he took a humongous tax deduction for the work. Must have been by some really important artist."

"Stocker has an almost mythical public image from his war service, so I would like a chance to tease out of the diary some details to enhance what we already know from the museum's files. Since I need to be back in the office starting tomorrow, it would be easier if I could examine the diary there."

"I'm sure Gabby won't like mind. Sorry, that made no sense. Gabby has been after me about how often I use the word 'like' in conversations, so I am trying to catch myself doing that. Anyway, as far as the diary is concerned, just in case, please leave a note in the file telling what you took, sign and date it and then I'll witness it."

Sam is removing the last of several very thick files from the top drawer of the fireproof file cabinet when an object drops out to land on her left foot.

"What the hell? Shit, that hurts. Oh, my God, it's a gun!" she exclaims as she hops around on her right foot while pointing at the offending revolver.

"Well, I'll be," Barnes says as he bends down to retrieve it. Popping out the magazine, Barnes continues, "It's not loaded.

Never seen one like this: 'Colt Automatic caliber .25' engraved on one side. Pretty light weight."

"Well, that damn thing is heavy enough to nearly break my foot," Sam moans as she hobbles over to her chair and plops down, the chair almost rolling out from under her as she did so. "Whoa!! 'Bout broke my ass to boot."

"Is there anything in those files to indicate if the pistol came out of one?"

"I don't know, Barnes. These are huge files. Most are marked 'Winfrey Estate.' It'll take days to go through these monsters," Sam grouses as she rubs her foot. "Wait, there's one with a hole in the bottom. It's labeled 'Tayler, Karson.' Tayler is spelled with an 'er,' and Karson with a 'K.'

"Most curious. I seem to recall that there was a physician in Freeport in the early 1900s named Karson Tayler. Spelled the same way. Though I think he committed suicide if I recall."

"Well, I'll put the gun back in the drawer and we can sort it out later."

"I'll do a little research on the gun," Barnes concludes as he makes a note of the gun's serial number.

Chapter 15

The second night the files are in The Raspitory, someone does gain access to the building. The security guard, responding to a noise at the back door, did not call for assistance before investigating. He is confronted by someone wearing a watch cap, a plaid scarf across the face, and holding a gun. When ordered to turn around, he is injected with a drug which renders him unconscious for more than eight hours. He is still "out" when the temp workers and Sam arrive the next morning.

Other than the obvious fact that some of the files had been opened, there is little to indicate that someone had spent the better part of four hours combing through them. Only when Sam examines the hard drives of the three computers does she find that someone has erased all their memories. The backup copy in the Weston and Sanderson vault and the one Sam carries with her insured that nothing is entirely lost, but Sam is both annoyed and worried about the security situation.

As added insurance after the break-in, at the end of each work day, Sam begins emailing a backup of the file to her sister in Chicago. Her sister is to delete the prior file once she receives a new one.

Gabby divides her days between the office and The Raspitory. The evening after the break-in she and Glenn work on the Bresch files after the temps and Sam leave for the day. About 8:00 p.m. Gabby receives a call just as she and Glenn are locking the security guard in for the night.

"Sam, what's up?"

"Barnes has been hurt. Someone beat him. He's unconscious."

"Where? When did this happen?"

"Museum, his office. Ambulance taking him to the hospital is leaving like now. Meet us at the ER." With that Sam is gone.

Tumbling Blocks

As Gabby begins to run towards her Wrangler, Glenn rushes to catch up, as he exclaims, "What the hell?"

"Barnes has been hurt. Someone beat him in his office. That was Sam. He's on the way to the hospital. We'll take my car, it'll save time."

"Geeze Louise Gertrude! How did Sam find out?"

"Don't know. She said she'd meet us in the ER."

Gabby pulls into the parking lot just as an ambulance arrives. Assuming it is Barnes, Gabby and Glenn enter through the visitor's entrance to inquire at the ER desk. The person on duty asks if Gabby is related to Harry Barnes.

"He goes by Elmer, his middle name, and I'm his attorney. He has no next of kin."

"And you?"

"I'm his architect—historical architect."

Never having had an attorney, or architect for that matter, of a patient try to see that patient in the ER, the clerk is not certain what to do.

"Please wait while I check on Mr. Barnes' status."

Less than two minutes later the clerk is back. "Mr. Barnes is still unconscious but a Samantha Greer asks that both of you be allowed to come back to see her."

"To see her? Is she a patient?"

"Yes, just arrived by ambulance."

"Shit and shoved in it."

"I beg your pardon."

"Sorry. Where do we go?"

By the time Gabby and Glenn arrive at the treatment bay where Sam is being examined, a female ER doctor is finishing a neural exam. As she walks out of the bay the physician says to the nurse, "Let's get a non-contrast CT of the head in bed six."

"Sam, what the hell happened?" Gabby begins as she takes Sam's hand.

Tumbling Blocks

"Hell, I don't know, but it hurts, oh, does it hurt. I was like supposed to go to H's for dinner, but when I got there like he wasn't. Thinking he'd be at the Museum, I walked over and went into his office. As I came through the door I saw him lying on the floor but some prick hit me from behind and knocked me down. Maybe I was even out for like a few seconds.

"When I could focus I saw the panic button for the alarm system hanging on the side of his desk, so I pressed it. Cops were there in just a couple minutes, I think, and then EMTs and an ambulance arrived. I insisted that H be taken first since he was still unconscious. While we waited for a second ambulance, I called you. Ahhh. This hurts! Someone's gotta go to H's house to let out poor Alfred Thayer. He's been in his crate since noon and will need relief. Glenn, can you go over to H's and do that?"

"H's place?"

"Barnes'."

"I'll go, but I don't have a key."

"There's one," Sam puts her hands to her temples, "ahhh shit, this really, really hurts. If I ever get my hands on the bastard who did this, I'll knock a turd outta him as long as a well rope. Geeze it smarts. Where was I, oh yeah, the key. To the right of the back door there is a large Chinese symbol—means 'peace' or some such shit. Anyway, there is a spare key in a pocket on the backside—bottom. Make sense?"

"I got it. If I have trouble, I'll call Gabby's cell," Glenn answers as he takes the Wrangler keys.

"Use of cell phones is not permitted in the ER," the nurse reminds them.

"OK, then I'll figure it out." With that Glenn is gone.

"Nurse, I'm also here for Dr. Barnes, so I would like to talk to the physician attending him when there is time."

"Are you family?"

"No. Dr. Barnes has no family or next of kin. I am his attorney, Gabriel Gordon."

"I'll let the doctor know you wish to speak with her."

53

Tumbling Blocks

After the nurse leaves, Gabby pulls a chair over to Sam's bed and again takes her hand. After a few minutes silence, Sam tries to turn her head toward Gabby, but pain stops her in mid-motion.

"Ahhh. Shit this hurts. Gabby, I suppose you're like wondering… Sorry, I know I'm supposed to stop with the 'likes,' but any way wondering about my knowing about the spare key and all?"

"Hadn't occurred to me yet, but I'd have gotten around to rethinking that part of the evening."

"H and I have become good friends. Don't freak out. We're not lovers or anything, just companions like. We spend a lot of time together. Ever since all the crap went down with the killing of Galway and all that mess, well, both of us were feeling…umm…kinda isolated. Not in a romantic sense, but just needing someone to talk to and hang with."

"So, 'H' is what you call him?"

"Yeah. Ohhhhh. It hurts to smile. He hates to be called Harry and I don't like Elmer, and Barnes is what everyone else calls him if they don't call him Dr. Barnes. So I latched onto the H thing. He seems to like it. We are supposed to go to Chicago in October to see like an opera. I've never seen one before, so he offered to take me." Sam pauses as she fights off another wave of pain.

"He's got season tickets. Always buys two seats so his wife can go. Says he thinks she won't mind if she doesn't go to this one. Isn't it sweet that he buys a season ticket for his deceased wife so that they can still share their love of opera? But this opera is by some dude named Verdi and she didn't like Italian opera too much. Ohhhh, geeze I'm gonna have ta do something if I don't get something for this headache. Any way, it's called 'Macbeth," the opera. It's about this crazy guy who kills lots of people to become a king. Sounds way cool."

Sam falls silent and Gabby can see that she is having trouble with the pain. Patting her hand, Gabby says, "You rest quietly for now. We can talk more later."

Tumbling Blocks

It is almost ten minutes before they come to take Sam for her
CT scan.

Chapter 16

s Sam is wheeled out of sight, Gabby heads to the
waiting room, stopping by the nurse's station to ask that
she be notified when either Dr. Barnes or Miss Greer is
brought back to the ER.

Sitting in the ER waiting room, Gabby replays in her
mind the conversation she just had with Sam and the revelation
of her deepening friendship with Barnes. She has to admit that
Glenn had been correct in his observation about Sam's attraction
to Barnes. And, she realizes, Sam's behavior has been changing
of late.

When Sam began working for Gabby there were some
pretty rough edges to the legal secretary. Sam was prone to drop
the f-bomb into her speech just like some people insert "uhms"
between phrases as they pause in their thinking. Except for
tonight when the pain of her head injury is unbearable, Sam's
use of scatological expletives has decreased markedly.

When they first met, Sam was always running late,
invariably due to some minor domestic crisis which had
elevated itself into a rational for being tardy. Sam seemed prone
to acquiring pets in much the same manner as a sweater attracts
pet fur. At one time Sam had a pet goat named Pinky that she
carted around in the back seat of her Civic, having removed the
seat cushion to allow Pinky to stand as she drove the creature
around town.

While Gabby was still unclear about the circumstances
under which Sam became the guardian of the goat, she recalled
that it had something to do with a practical joke of the goat
being placed on the balcony of someone's apartment. At the feet
of Pinky were several chewed books and a movie film canister
with some pieces of film also gnawed on. The unwitting goat
was equipped with a sign hanging from its neck which read, "I
liked the book better."

Gabby is smiling to herself as she recalls the story of
Pinky. She realizes that she never knew how Sam disposed on

the bovid ruminate; a topic for a discussion later. Her reverie is interrupted when the receptionist informs her that Dr. Barnes is back in the ER.

Chapter 17

F inding Barnes in the ER bay next to Sam's, Gabby goes over to the bed and takes his hand. His head is wrapped in an enormous bandage. He looks at Gabby but does not speak. She can see the pain in his eyes as he is struggling to refrain from any outburst that he would later consider to have been ungentlemanly. Gabby begins brushing the graying hair back from his temple when the nurse and doctor come in.

"Doctor, this is Gabriel Gordon, Mr. Barnes' attorney."

"Hello, I am Doctor Archana Vaidya," the 5' 5" Indian woman says in a clear Midwestern accent. "Does Mr. Barnes have an advance directive or do you have power of attorney for health care?"

Gabby's heart leaps into her throat at the doctor's words. She turns to look at Barnes.

"Oh, I am sorry, Miss Gordon, I did not mean to imply that Mr. Barnes is terminal. I just need some assurance that I can speak with you under HIPAA."

"I do have power of attorney for health care. I can provide you with a copy. It's in my office files. Do you need it immediately?"

"No. Dr. Barnes is it OK with you if I discuss your case with Miss Gordon?"

Barnes nods his head slightly indicating his assent. Turning to Gabby, Dr. Vaidya says, "Still, it would be best if you can bring in a copy of the power of attorney for healthcare tomorrow. That way it will become part of his file here. Now, as to his condition, we'll keep him overnight for observation. The CT shows that there is a hairline fracture of the skull. He does have a concussion but we want to be certain that there was no contrecoup damage to the brain. He will need to rest for several weeks before getting back to full activity. There is also a laceration on the top of his head. Whatever his assailant hit him with took out about a three inch diameter piece of his scalp. Is he retired?"

"Yes and no. He's director of the Stephenson County Museum, but he retired from the Smithsonian several years ago and then moved back here. That's when he took the local job."

"Does he live alone?"

"Yes, his wife passed away a couple years before he moved back. But we can arrange for him to have someone there all the time. He has several very close friends who will be glad to help."

"Are there stairs in his home?"

"Yes. Dr. Barnes' bedroom is on the second floor. But we can arrange something for him on the ground floor."

"You seem pretty familiar with his living arrangements for being his attorney."

"We are also very good friends. We have dinner together at each other's homes almost every week."

"Well, when we are ready to send him home, we'll want to make sure that all of these details are worked out."

"Doctor Vaidya, how long was he unconscious?"

"He gained consciousness right before the CT. He was very coherent but in lots of pain. We've given him a mild pain killer. We need him coherent to check for any undetected bleeding inside his skull. As a result we do not want to sedate him too heavily. They should have a bed ready for him soon on one of the floors."

"Thank you, doctor. And what about my friend Samantha Greer?"

"Power of Attorney for Health Care?"

"Yes, as a matter of fact."

"I've yet to see the results of her CT, but given that she also has head trauma, we'll want to keep her overnight for observation at least."

Glenn returns from his mission of mercy on behalf of Alfred Thayer, the Welsh Corgi belonging to Barnes. Just as Barnes is being taken up to his room Sam arrives back in the ER. The three of them wait for the processing to get her a bed for the night. To Gabby's surprise, Sam does not fight the

59

doctor's order that she stay the night. The fact that she has just been given a pain killer could have been the reason for Sam's uncharacteristic docility.

Chapter 18

W hen Gabby arrives at Barnes' hospital room the next
morning, he is fully conscious and seems to be in
good spirits.

"My dear, how nice of you to come see me. But you've
got things to do. Don't waste time on an aging bibliophile."

"I'll hear none of that. You are officially under the care
of the Glenn and Gabby health care system until further notice.
Sarah Fuller will be in to see you today so that she can
coordinate your post-hospital care," Gabby says as she gives
Barnes a hug. "How are you feeling? That's one huge bandage."

"Perennial problem with scalp wounds...no place to
stick the bandages if there is hair. So they have to wrap one up
like a water chestnut inside a slice of bacon at a cocktail party,
sans the toothpick, of course. Though it feels like someone stuck
one through my head last night."

"It seems you've not lost your sense of humor."

"Well, the pain in my head comes in waves, so there are
times when I might be downright misanthropic. From what the
physician told me this morning, I'll have a very noticeable but
almost perfect tonsure. Funny, I never saw myself as a
Franciscan. An Augustinian perhaps, but not a Franciscan."

"Have the police been in to interview you?"

"No, I expect them any time, though I don't think I can
tell them much."

"Well, we're just happy that you're OK and everything
can be mended. Can I get you anything?"

"I would positively give up another divot from my
adamantine skull for a decent cup of tea."

"I'll see if the cafeteria can manage that. I know: two
sugars and milk, not cream."

Gabby is headed for the elevator when she sees
Detectives Mark Sumner and Dave Winslow coming down the
hall. Detective Sumner was involved in the investigation into the

murder of Galway, as well as the aftermath of the shoot-out at Babcook Manor two years prior.

"Detectives, how have you been?" Gabby extends her hand.

"Doing well, Miss Gordon. And you?" Sumner replies as he takes her hand.

"I'd be better if I didn't have two friends here as a result of someone whacking them over the head."

"Ohhh. So you're a friend of both Dr. Barnes and Miss Greer?" Detective Winslow asks.

"Yes. Miss Greer works for me and Dr. Barnes has been aiding us in organizing the files from the Bresch Building."

"Well, we're on our way to interview Dr. Barnes."

"May I join you?"

"As his friend or his attorney?" Sumner queries.

"Does he need an attorney?"

"Not that I know of. So we'll say you're here as his friend then."

Back in Barnes' room the detectives asks for a detailed description of what happened.

"Well, I'm afraid my memory is groggy at best. Let's see. I was just getting ready to head home. I'd been scanning documents into the computer and I dropped my favorite pen—a fountain pen that was an anniversary gift from my wife—and I bent down to get it. That is the last I remember until I regained consciousness in the testing area here in the hospital."

"See anyone hanging around outside the museum?"

"No. The docent left at four after closing up the museum itself. I was in the Carriage House, which is where my office is located."

"Do you keep the door to the Carriage House locked?"

"Not during regular hours. When I work late at night or on days we're closed, then I lock the outside door. Last night, however, I was in a rush to complete a project before heading home to meet Miss Greer, so I neglected to lock the door after the docent left."

"The doctor's report says you were hit twice. The first blow was from behind and was probably lessened when you bent over for the pen. The second blow was after you were on the floor, probably already unconscious," Sumner explains.

"Were we being robbed?"

"Some of your staff came in to the museum early this morning but could not find anything missing. Just a big mess as someone had ransacked the place. But nothing of value appears to have been taken. Well, Dr. Barnes, if you remember anything else about the assault, please don't hesitate to contact me." Sumner hands Barnes a business card as he prepares to leave.

"Detective, do you think Dr. Barnes will be safe in his own home after this?" Gabby queries.

"Oh, dear," Barnes begins. "Let's not start thinking along those lines. I feel certain this was some misguided lad looking for a quick score for drug money. That would explain the offices being torn up. Looking for cash or something with street value to fence. Museums are not good places for such booty. Anyone with any sense of the value of museum artifacts would not be inclined to throw things around so carelessly."

"You're probably right, Doctor," Sumner responds. "No, Miss Gordon, I doubt that whoever attacked Doctor Barnes was after him personally. He was just in the wrong place at the wrong time."

With that Sumner and Winslow leave.

Chapter 19

S orting and cataloging all of the files is a slow process, but by the end of the fourth week it is pretty much complete. Gabby's law firm of Weston and Sanderson is fielding ten to fifteen calls per day from people who think they ought to have something important in the files. As the office manager Emma notes, "Seventy percent of the calls are from the same people calling back again and again. What part of 'we'll call you as soon as we know' don't they get? I want to keep a log of who calls and how often so that the first person we call back will be the person who called us the least often."

As the file sorting process is progressing Gabby meets with Joe Shenk, who had made his appointment soon after the vault was discovered. At sixty-two, Joe is a maintenance worker for Freeport School District. When he arrives for the 3:00 p.m. appointment he is still wearing his uniform shirt adorned with both the district's logo and his name badge. Gabby thinks he looks tired and worn down--as if the world has defeated him day after day for his entire life.

"Good afternoon, Mr. Shenk. Please have a seat," Gabby begins as they shake hands in her office. "What can we do for you?"

"I have no money to pay for anything, but I am praying that in the files of the Bresches there may be information about my great grandfather's estate."

"Did the Bresches handle the estate?"

"Yeah, old man Bresch, that is the first Bresch, wrote the Will, including the terms of the…whadya call it…inheritance, yeah, that's it, inheritance left by Jeremiah Winfrey, who was my great grandfather."

"Are you interested in the paper work just for family history or is there another reason you wish to have the file?"

"My dad was never allowed to see the actual Will. He died believing that there was something crooked with the whole deal."

"Well, Mr. Shenk, the paperwork, all of it, legally belongs to you if you can prove direct descent. Now any paperwork in the files, such as notes by Bresch, would not belong to you."

"There were two law suits, one that my granddad started, and then one my dad filed. Both trying to get the Will overturned, but they never got a trial. They used every dime they had trying to set things right."

"Did they have some specific concerns about the Estate?"

"Great grandfather pretty much left his children out of his Will. That would have been my grandfather. Most of the money was to go to the grandkids after old man Winfrey's kids died. But when all was said and done, the Bresches told us there was no money left. Grandpa and Dad always thought the whole thing was not right. For one thing, Winfrey had dozens and dozens of patents. What happened to all the money they should have generated?"

"Now that I think about it, there are several very large files labeled 'Winfrey Estate.' I will have our staff try to determine what is yours and then we'll call you. I believe we have your number."

"Thank you, Miss Gordon. You're very kind. I appreciate you taking time to see me without charging for your time."

"Miss Zangara will show you out."

After her meeting with Shenk, Gabby heads over to The Raspitory where four women are working under Sam's supervision sorting and indexing the files.

"Sam, you recall seeing a couple big files labeled 'Winfrey Estate?' Gabby asks as she enters.

Tumbling Blocks

"Just a sec," Sam responds as she begins tapping the keys of her laptop. "Yep, they're in box four-four-two. Should be along the north wall, about half-way down."

Gabby walks down the line of boxes until she finds 442. Opening the lid she sees that the entire box is taken up with files all labeled "Winfrey Trust." Hefting the unexpectedly heavy box she lugs it over to any empty table and pulls out the file which looks to be the oldest. As she begins leafing through the hand written documents she flips open her cell and hits Barnes' home number on her speed dial list.

"Hello, Barnes here."

"Doc, how are you?"

"Well, Gabby, what a pleasant surprise. I'm fine. How are you?" responds the cheerful voice on the other end.

"I'm very well. And how's your head getting along?"

"Anxious to get back to work. I hope my physician will release me tomorrow when I meet with him."

"Well, don't push it. They don't give out medals for pain and suffering if they are self-inflicted."

"I understand, but I am slowly going crazy being forced to stay away from work. I've been taking walks like the doctor ordered, but now poor Alfred Thayer hides from me because I've taken him for so many walks he's beginning to lose weight."

"Nevertheless, don't push the doctor into a premature release."

"I have been warned. Is there something else you wanted?"

"Actually, there is. What can you tell me about Jeremiah Winfrey? I recall that name from somewhere."

"Oh, let's see. Not to be unkind, but old man Winfrey was a twenty-four-carat-gold- plated-purple-revolving bastard. But I think I better refer you to Harriett. She writes that weekly local history column in the *Journal Standard*. Last year she did a three-part series on the Winfreys. She'll be more up on them.

66

Tell her I told you to call. By the way, are we still on for dinner tomorrow night?"

"Of course. Sam says she'll drive you over. So, we'll see you then and hopefully, you'll have news from the doctor."

"Good news I hope. Cheerio."

Chapter 20

H arriett turns out to be a veritable fountain of information once Gabby gets her talking.

"Well, let me think where to start," she begins her tale. "Winfrey was a one-man industrial revolution. He held over one-hundred-twenty patents and most of them made money. When he died in 1918 he was the richest man in Illinois."

"We've got numerous files from the Bresch law firm on the Winfrey Estate. Before I go digging through them, I am curious as to why it generated so much paperwork and litigation?"

"Well, he was extremely hard working and had no tolerance for anyone who did not share his work ethic. Of course, neither of his children could hope to live up to his standards, so he was estranged from them well before the time he died. His estate was not to be distributed to grandchildren until they had reached the age of sixty-five and all their parents were deceased."

"Wow! Talk about tying up a legacy."

"It was because of Jeremiah Winfrey and a guy named Marshall Field that Illinois passed laws which today govern how far out an estate can be controlled from the grave."

"Have you ever seen any figures on how much the estate was worth at the time of his death?"

"The papers at the time estimated that it was in the neighborhood of six million. And that was in nineteen-twenty. Then there would have been the on-going revenue from licensing his patents. What brought up the Winfrey estate?"

"A man claiming to be his great grandson came to see me today asking for access to the papers."

"I had no idea anyone was still alive. Does he live in Freeport?"

"Probably. He says his father always believed that the Bresches were manipulating the terms of the Will. If there is a case there, then he could become a client, so at this time I better not reveal his name. I guess I'll have to do some homework and read my way through these files."

"If there is anything else with which I may help, please let me know."

Chapter 21

G abby and Sam spend the next day working their way through the Winfrey papers. At about 3 p.m. Sam motions for Gabby to come with her outside the Raspitory. Once standing on the sidewalk, she starts, "I didn't want the temps to like actually hear this conversation, since I do not know how much we can trust them with private information."

"Probably a good idea to be careful. They did sign confidentiality statements, but they may not have any understanding about the legal implications of revealing anything they have seen. I'll make a point of reinforcing that before they leave today."

"I don't know what you've found, but in the files I've read, the Bresches were like ripping off the Winfrey account for huge chunks of change. Old man Bresch was the Executor of the Estate, so he called all the shots. The fees they charged against the Estate for defending against the family's suits and for managing the funds were like enormous." Sam is becoming agitated as she relates her findings. Gabby takes Sam's arm to pull her in closer to the building in what appears to be an effort to keep passers-by from hearing. What she is really doing is trying to calm her secretary and to get them into the shade of the building, the heat of the late July afternoon sun beating down mercilessly.

"I've not seen any of the financial data," Gabby adds, "but I haven't seen anything which would suggest that the Winfrey Will was that air tight. Mr. Shenk said that the suits his father and grandfather filed never even got to the trial phases."

"If we can actually find records of those suits, it may be interesting to compare the names of the attorneys with the accounts payable. Actually the Estate was paying healthy sums to like a couple out-of-town attorneys for no apparent reason."

Tumbling Blocks

"How much would you guess the Bresches bilked out of the Estate?" Gabby asks as both of them glance over at the vacant lot and the now empty vault tower.

"Well, the initial probate showed the total value of the Estate at a little over six million. There was regular income from like the patent licenses in the neighborhood of a hundred grand a year up to about 1930. Then they sold off most of the licenses for like very low fees considering the regular income they were generating. Bottom line--when the Estate paid off the grandkids, there was something less than a half million left."

"Wow! Even if the funds were invested in simple savings accounts, the interest generated plus the patent fees ought to have covered normal Executor and legal fees. This case is beginning to take on a sense of the surreal."

"What I don't see is like why it took so long to pay off the grandkids."

"Old man Winfrey's youngest child lived to the ripe old age of ninety-two. By that time all of the grandkids were dead. I found notes which stated that efforts to find the great grandkids were actually unsuccessful, but the Bresches were skimming off big fees even as they made minimal effort to find the heirs."

"What makes even less sense is that Joe Shenk told me that his family has never gotten any money from the Estate. Did the Bresches manage to keep all of it away from the family?"

"If that's the case, then like where did all the money go? It's not like the Bresches were living an overly lavish lifestyle. Maybe there is like a vacation home in the Caribbean or something."

"Tomorrow I'll tackle the files with the firm's accounts. Maybe that'll give us some answers."

Chapter 22

B etty Bresch is surprised then angered to see two Freeport police detectives standing at her front door when she responds to her doorbell.

"Now what do you guys want?"

"Sorry to bother you ma'am. I'm Detective Mark Sumner and this is Detective Dave Winslow. We may have new information about your late husband. Do you mind if we come in?"

"What about the pig? You still think I had something to do with his disappearance? This is really getting old," Betty carps as she steps back for the detectives to enter her home.

"No, ma'am," Winslow responds. "We have new information about Mr. Bresch."

"You mean you've found the bastard?"

"Perhaps," Sumner begins. "We received information from the Conway County, Arkansas sheriff's office that a 1978 Oldsmobile Ninety-eight Regency with Illinois plates matching those of your husband's was recently retrieved from the Arkansas River."

"Arkansas? Why the hell would he have been there?"

"We don't know, ma'am. The remains of two people, one male and one female were inside. They are awaiting dental records to confirm identities, but if you would happen to have anything containing your husband's DNA, like a hair brush or toothbrush, that might help. Perhaps we could get a sample from one of your children?"

"Anything I had that belonged to that son of a bitch was burned long ago. And I doubt that either of his kids would care enough to take the time to give you the skin off their teeth, let alone anything else."

"We were also informed that the VIN on the car matches the one you reported missing."

"How the hell did they end up in a river, not that I care who or what took out his sorry ass?"

Tumbling Blocks

"According to the Conway sheriff, in mid-June of 1980, which is when the car was reported missing, they were experiencing a period of heavy rains and the river was well above flood stage."

"Speculation is that they exited I-40 looking for gas or some…"

"Or a place to shack-up."

"…or something, and missed a turn, plunging into the river. The high current swept the car downstream until it snagged on something and then dropped to the bottom as it filled with water."

"The recent years of drought in the south lowered the river level to the point that someone fishing along that stretch of river spotted a small portion of the car above water and called the sheriff."

"Well, that's the wildest thing I've ever heard. Serves the old turd right getting drowned in muddy water. Were they able to recover any of his belongings?"

"The report says there was luggage in the trunk. Most of it was rotted, but they did locate a set of papers in a zip seal plastic bag which managed to stay dry all these years. Copies of the papers will be sent to you, but the originals will be kept as evidence."

"Evidence of what?"

"They'll probably hang on to the stuff for a couple years as a precaution in the event something might indicate that this was something other than an accident. I would imagine that if you find anything in the copies which would cause you to want the originals, you'd have to get a judge down there to order the release."

"Just what I need, more lawyers to kick me around. Is there anything else?"

"No, ma'am. We just wanted to deliver the news in person rather than by a phone call. If you have any questions, here's my card."

Tumbling Blocks

After Betty closes the door she dances a jig down the hall singing, "Yes, oh yes, dead, dead, the bastard IS dead, the sick bastard's dead."

Chapter 23

Outside, as the two detectives get in their car, Mark comments, "She sure wasn't upset about being told her husband is confirmed dead. Maybe the guys who investigated the case thirty years ago where right in suspecting her. Might be worth another look at the evidence."

"Sorta reminds me of that noir film 'Double Indenture'..."

"Double Indemnity."

"Yeah, that's it. The one with Barbara Streisand..."

"Barbara Stanwyck," Sumner corrected. Winslow's love of classic films frequently trips up on his inability to remember anything factual about them.

"Yeah and that guy, oh, what was his name? Played William Frawley on 'My Three Sons'?"

"William Frawley was an actor on 'My Three Sons'!"

"Yeah, and he was Fred Mernitz on 'I Love Lucy'."

"Fred Mertz."

"He was Uncle Charley on 'My Three Sons'."

"William Demarest played Uncle Charley after William Frawley died."

"Oh."

"Frawley played Bud."

"Whatever. But anyway, there was this woman who killed her husband for the insurance money and the guy from 'My Three Sons'..."

"Fred MacMurray."

"Yeah, that's him. He was some insurance investigator or something. I think they named a college after him."

"The insurance agent?"

"No, well yeah, the MacMurphy guy."

"MacMurray."

"Yeah. Say, how come you know so much about this stuff? You said you never watch TV or movies."

"Well, I have been around some, you know?"

Tumbling Blocks

"Well, anyway, my point was that did anyone take a look at this Bresch lady visa-visa her dearly departed husband's life insurance?"

Pulling the case file from his briefcase, Sumner thumbed through it until he found the papers he wanted. "The file shows that the insurance company was the prime reason it took so long to have him declared legally dead. They wanted time to make sure there was nothing untoward about the death."

"Well, it might be toward for a second look."

"Couldn't hurt."

After a pause, Winslow adds, "He was also in a Disney flick called 'Flipper'?"

"'Flubber'."

"Something like that."

Chapter 24

The next morning, a bright July day with blue skies and rising humidity, Sam is walking the two blocks from her parked car to the Raspitory when someone comes out from between two buildings, knocks her to the ground and grabs her purse. She barely catches a glimpse of her attacker before he disappears around the corner and down the alley.

The police later find her purse in a dumpster, but nothing is missing. Discussing the incident later with Gabby they conclude that the attacker was after the portable memory stick Sam carries with the back-up of the Bresch files. What the attacker did not know is that Sam wears it on a lanyard around her neck.

The discussion with the police leads to further speculation that the attacker may have learned about Sam carrying a back-up of the computer files from one of the temp workers at the Raspitory. Detective Winslow asks for and is given the names of the temp workers so that he can run a background check on each one.

"This whole thing is getting too dangerous," Gabby insists while talking with Sam later. "From now on none of us will go anywhere alone. Maybe you ought to move out to Babcook Manor for the time being."

"Then what about H? He's living alone and Glenn has those long drives back to Madison like every night," Sam offers.

"Good point. Though Glenn will soon stop coming down except on weekends as he's exhausted the patience of his employer with all the time he's taken off because of this whole misadventure."

"That still leaves H going solo."

"Well, there is certainly enough room at Babcook for him."

"You really think you'll get him to like stay there, even for a week or two?"

"Somehow I doubt it. I'll call Detective Sumner to see what he thinks about the Doc's safety."

"Simplest solution would be for me to like move in with H, but that'd leave you alone."

"I'm not worried about me. The Manor has an alarm system, I do have a gun, and Alys, Sarah and Irish Red are close by. Do you think staying at Doc's would be acceptable to him?"

"All we can do is to like ask. I'll present it as the alternative to him moving to the Manor."
The conversation with Barnes goes better than Sam and Gabby had hoped.

"Ladies, I appreciate your concern for my safety, but I am not about to decamp my comfortable digs. Besides, I've got Alfred Thayer Mahan to warn off any would be intruders. Now, as to Samantha staying here, she would always be a welcome guest and great company. But I will leave that decision up to her, as my door is always open."

"That's very gracious of you, H. Are you sure that you and Alfred Thayer aren't too set in your bachelor ways to like have a female invading your space?"

"Of course not. We'd be glad of the company and we have an extra bedroom with *en suite* facilities. And to be honest, we may become bothersome for you since our custom is to listen to classical music while we cook."

"What sort of music? Opera?" Sam questions cautiously.

"Generally not opera. They are too long to get through a complete one while preparing a meal. We're partial to the 'B's."

"The 'B's?"

"Bach, Beethoven, Brahms."

"Are there other letters?"

"Well, not to be judgmental, but we generally dislike the 'S's. Sciabin, Schoenberg, and Stravinsky. Too grating for Alfred Thayer's ears."

"Well, I'll just like use my I-Pod and ear buds so I can stick with the 'K's—Toby Keith, Keith Urban and Kenny Rogers."

Chapter 25

G abby is surprised when detectives Sumner and Winslow show up at her office soon after Sam begins staying with Barnes.

"We've been doing some digging into the Bresch case and wanted to compare some notes with you," Sumner begins.

"I'll be glad to share what I know," Gabby offers.

"Good," Winslow continues. "There was a letter to Mrs. Bresch from her husband. It was postmarked from St. Louis a day after she says she realized something had happened to him. The letter said he was 'OK' and told her not to ever worry about him again."

"The fact that she did not inform the police about her husband's disappearance until five days after the last time she saw or talked to him made the detectives suspicious at the time. Then when she finally revealed the fact that she had received a letter from him, suspicions ran even higher," Winslow reports.

"However, the guys working the case were not able to find a single piece of evidence connecting her to either the disappearance or to the missing money," Sumner expands.

"You may be interested to know that Bresch did not take money from his firm's trust account. He left that intact. In fact, our files have copies of court records which show that everyone who had money held by the Bresch law firm eventually got repaid, if they could prove their right to the funds."

"But there were a number of people who claimed to have paid Bresch retainers or other funds, but had no way of proving it. These were the few unfortunate folks who claimed to have paid funds to the firm, but had neither cancelled checks nor receipts to substantiate their claims," Sumner concludes.

"So," Gabby queries, "what happened to the funds in the trust account that the court did not order returned?"

"After ten years Mrs. Bresch was allowed to have the money on condition that she find two other law firms in Freeport that would agree to be good for the money if any future claims could be substantiated and she could not pay those claims," answers Sumner.

"So, how much did she get from the trust fund?"

"Twenty-eight thousand and some change," Winslow responds.

"What firms vouched for the repayment?"

"Both were individual practices that closed within eight years of vouching for the money. In both cases the attorney retired," Sumner says with raised eyebrows which expressed his disbelief that all this was purely coincidental.

"I can't believe that there was enough money left in the trust fund to induce someone to take the risk of vouching for Bitter Betty if they felt that she was not going to be around if the axe fell," opines Gabby.

"That's what we thought, but who knows what type of pressure she put on the two guys," counters Winslow.

"But wait, there should have been several million in that trust from the Winfrey Estate," Gabby asserts.

"Nothing like that showed up in the court records," Sumner attests, his instincts further aroused. "What was the Winfrey Estate?"

Gabby gives a brief summary of the history of the Winfrey estate, as well as the string of facts she and Sam have uncovered from the Bresch files.

"I suppose with the files of the firm missing at the time it was impossible to have an audit performed. Winfrey had been dead long enough that no one probably even considered the fact that the firm should have held funds from his estate, except for his descendants, who were never informed that they had money coming," Gabby pronounces.

"We certainly had no idea about that until talking to you, and it is obvious that the original investigators were unaware of that fact," Sumner adds as he closes the file folder in front of him.

Tumbling Blocks

"Did Nick Bresch somehow manage to get the Winfrey money out of the bank account that held his practice's trust fund?" Gabby says after thinking for a few minutes.

"According to the notes in the case file, the Bresch trust fund was invested at First National Bank. I think that's Fifth/Third Bank today," Sumner notes. "The records of that account were subpoenaed and it showed that there had not been any suspicious activity within years of Bresch's disappearance."

"So, the Winfrey money was parked in some other bank account not identified as a trust account," Gabby further speculates.

"You've been through the firms internal records, how did he record the Winfrey Estate?" Winslow solicits.

"It shows up as part of the records of client funds which the firm held, but come to think of it, we have not examined their firm's actual bank statements. I think that's where we need to go next. We'll keep you apprised of whatever we uncover," Gabby concludes.

"Well, if you need help or some expertise on this, we can have a forensic accountant from the state crime lab give you a hand," Sumner offers as the two officers rise to leave.

Chapter 26

Once in their unmarked police car, Winslow opines, "You know this Bresch gal is like one of them femmy fatals. Like in 'Murder, My Swede.'"

"It's 'femme fatale,' and 'Murder, My Sweet.'"

"Oh, yeah. And like that gal in 'The Maltese Falcon.' What was her name…? Yeah, Mary Nastor."

"No, Mary Astor. Played Brigid O'Shaughnessy."

"Tried to lure Bogie into a life of crime and then she was going to knock him off. What was his character's name? Sam Scoop."

"Sam Spade."

"And then there was a femmy fatale in …"

"Femme fatale."

"In "Duel in the Summer."

"'Duel in the Sun.'"

"Oh. Well, you know. The actress was Jennifer Smith…"

"Jones."

"Same difference. Anyway, this Bresch gal is like one of them gals. Luring men to their deaths. Kinda like a black widow spider. 'Step into my web said the spider to the fly.'"

"'Walk into my parlor said the spider to the fly.'"

"Same difference."

"Remind me never to rely on you for testimony in case I am accused of a crime," Sumner retorts as he turns on the car's ignition.

Chapter 27

For lunch that same day Gabby takes Sam to This Is It Eatery, a new restaurant in town that had opened just the prior October. Since it is Sam's birthday, Gabby's pleased to have an excuse to eat at Freeport's latest locale where one can observe "the ladies who lunch."

At first they begin discussing the Bresch case, but decide that the closeness of the tables precludes such a discussion lest they be overheard. Their food has just been delivered when Gabby notices out of the corner of her eye a man headed to their table.

"Counselor Gordon," the short, thin man with gray hair intones as he approaches.

Gabby stands as she extends her hand as she greets, "Mr. Bogusz, nice to see you."

"Sorry to interrupt, ladies, but I wanted to ask if you would be willing to serve on a new advisory committee for the mayor. We are going to develop a strategic vision for the city and try to lay out some sort of priority list."

"I'll take it under advisement, but you must understand that I am very busy with all the work surrounding the Bresch Building."

"Oh, I know, but I am sure you can appreciate the need for the city to have a vision of where we need to go in order to begin to turn around things, economically speaking."

"I am sympathetic, but really need to think about such a commitment."

"Well, I'll put you on our email list and make sure you get all of the pre-meeting documents, as well as notices of our preliminary planning sessions."

"No promises," Gabby asserts with a stern look on her face.

"OK, then, I'll leave you two to your lunch and I look forward to getting feedback on our plans." With that Dick Bogusz walks away.

After Gabby sits down, a silence ensues as each woman begins to eat.

Sam finally breaks the quiet as she tentatively approaches a new topic. "So, when are you and Glenn going to tie the knot?"

"That's a good question. We're waiting on Glenn's annulment, which seems to have gotten caught in some bureaucratic mess."

"I guess my non-Catholic head has a hard time comprehending all this. I thought your church does not recognize divorce."

"I'm no expert on Church law, but a divorce is a dissolution of a marriage by a civil court. And, yes, the Catholic Church does not recognize them. However, the Church does and can declare a marriage annulled if there are circumstances which existed prior to the marriage which make the marriage invalid to begin with."

"Sounds way too complicated for me."

"In my case, Tom was unfaithful, which was grounds for a divorce. However, because he admitted to the Marriage Tribunal that he entered our marriage with the intent of never being faithful, even admitting that he was cheating on me while we were engaged, the Tribunal determined that his vows at our wedding were not valid and therefore our marriage was invalid."

"But what about Glenn's?"

"That's the puzzler. Glenn was never baptized a Christian, let alone a Catholic, nor was his wife. They were not married in any type of Christian ceremony. Now that Glenn has become a Catholic, having his first marriage annulled is supposed to be a simple process. He was informed a few weeks ago that there was some problem with his petition for the annulment and that the process has been put on hold."

"That seems unfair. I can see that a church could say to its members that if you marry here you've got to follow our rules, but how can they hold someone accountable for obeying rules they never agreed to?"

"That's what we think. Making me and Tom seek an annulment is justified because I was married within the Church and knew all the rules. Glenn, however, is being held hostage to rules he never knew existed at the time he was married."

"So, you're on hold waiting for this Tribunal thing to like get its act together."

"That about sums it up."

"Any way to appeal the process?"

"We're talking about making an appointment with the pastor of Glenn's parish in Madison to see if there is anything else we can do. I've even begun looking into hiring a canon lawyer to handle the case."

"Like a lawyer with a gun—cannon?"

"No, Canon Law is the name of the body of rules which govern the Catholic Church. A canon lawyer is someone who specializes in such laws. They don't operate in civil or criminal courts like we do. Just inside the Church's bureaucracy."

"That sounds like a real fun profession."

Their discussion of annulments and canon lawyers is cut short with the delivery of two deep fried Oreos to their table.

Chapter 28

The next day Gabby puts Sam on the task of tracking the bank accounts of the Bresch law firm. The files are readily located among the myriad of files and records recovered from the vault. Soon Sam is reporting back to Gabby on her cursory audit.

"They were pretty smart bastards," Sam begins. "From the beginning, the Winfrey Estate was not listed in any bank accounts locally. Chicago Mercantile and Trust held that account, which is where old man Winfrey had an account when he died. It looks like Winfrey just kept the estate's money there, transferring the name on the account from Winfrey to Bresch. That account was never identified in any paperwork with the bank as being an attorney trust account."

"When did old man Winfrey die?" Gabby asks.

"Nineteen twenty."

"That explains it. The Bresch firm got its hands on the Winfrey money before Illinois laws began requiring law firms to keep client money separate from the law firm's money. Today we have operating accounts for payroll, rent, etc., which is the firm's money, and then there must be a trust account in which client money is held. So, for example, if a client pays us a retainer, that money is held in the trust account until the client is billed for services. Then funds are withdrawn from the trust fund to be placed in our firm's operating fund."

"In other words, the Bresches managed to hide the Winfrey Estate by never declaring to the Chicago bank the true nature of the funds."

"So it was from that account that Nick Bresch transferred money into another account?" Gabby asks.

"Right, but get this. I was able to find records that show that Nick transferred to that Chicago account funds from his office operating account and from his personal accounts, those were joint accounts with Bitter Betty. But then he transferred the whole lot into a Grand Cayman bank. Those transfers to the

Chicago account were made over several months and were completed four months before he disappeared," explains Sam.

"If he had waited until the very last minute to make those transfers, the police probably would have found the account when the bank mailed a closing statement to the firm. Either Nick or Shiloh were pretty smart when it came to all this—they closed the account far enough ahead of their leaving that they did not have to worry about a final bank statement showing up after they left that would give away what they did. If we hadn't found these really old records and then traced the account forward, no one would have ever know what these two had done. And with the files hidden for thirty years, none of the folks looking at the Bresch accounts had a clue about the Chicago account, let alone all the transfers to an off-shore bank."

"Well, in the early eighties, they did not have the sophisticated electronic transfers we have today. Nick probably wanted to make sure the money got to the Grand Cayman bank before they split. Would have been embarrassing to get down there and then find out that the millions you thought were your nest egg had been held up somewhere," Gabby speculates as she stares off into space thinking about the mentality of Bresch.

Chapter 29

After Emily Zangara fields a call from Thomas Buckle asking for an appointment to see Gabby about materials he thought were in the Bresch files, she calls Sam at the Raspitory to see if anyone has located a file under that name. The next afternoon, when Mr. Buckle enters Gabby's office she has the file on her desk, having just finished reading it. Thomas is 5' 5' with a nearly bald pate, which seems even balder because the hair remaining is completely white. He has an oval face, is slightly stooped at the shoulders, but otherwise very fit and trim for a man in his late eighties.

"Mr. Buckle, it is so nice to meet you. Please have a seat."

"Miss Gordon, thank you so much for seeing me," he replies in a very pleasant tone with what Gabby thinks is an English accent.

"Would you like a cup of coffee, glass of water, or a can of pop?"

"No, thank you. I wouldn't mind a cup of tea, but I am sure you don't have…"

"Milk?"

"Why, yes. Americans seem to think that putting cream in tea is no different than putting it in coffee, but there is a huge difference."

"I deduced from your accent that you would like your tea more in keeping with your native lands." Going to her door, Gabby asks Emily to bring Mr. Buckle a cup of strongly brewed tea with milk and "one or two sugars?"

"Three, if you please."

Seated at the conference table, the two chat about the weather until Emily returns with the requested cup of tea. After Emily leaves, Gabby begins.

"I see from your file that you asked Mr. Bresch to file a suit against your neighbor, Leo Ranken."

"In truth, its Leopold von Ranke, the 'e' on the end is pronounced like 'ah'."

"I see."

"He uses the name Leo Ranken today. He tries to hide his identity. He was a Nazi during the Great War of Nineteen-thirty-nine to Nineteen-forty-five."

"I see. And you were suing him because the fence he erected between your two properties was in fact on your land. That was your claim?"

"Yes, Ma'am, it is a fact."

"I see here that you began meeting with Mr. Bresch in late 1979 and that Mr. Bresch was about to file your suit just before he disappeared in 1980. Do I have the facts straight?"

"That is correct."

"So, how was your suit resolved?"

"It was never filed."

"Then you didn't go to another attorney?"

"No, I have been waiting for redress from the original suit."

"But Mr. Buckle, until the suit is filed, the court cannot act on it."

"As you might guess, I can be a very patient man."

"But if the Bresch files had not been found, your suit would never have made it to court."

"But they have been found and now I want to proceed."

"After all these years, does Mr. Ranken still live next to you?"

"I regret to say that indeed he does."

"Is the fence still there and in the wrong place?"

"Yes, the dastardly thing is still there, though von Ranke replaced all of it with pressure treated wood about fifteen years ago. But the new fence was placed exactly where the old fence stood."

"I do not see in the files anything which indicates that you had surveyors or engineers mark the actually property line."

"No need to. I know the fence is on my land and that man must be made to remove it."

"How do know that?"

"Miss Gordon, do you know what a Right of Way marker is?"

"No."

"It is a concrete post placed in the ground by the state and county to mark the legal boundaries of roads and highways. They sometimes have the letters R.O.W. on them."

"And how does a Right of Way marker bear on your case?"

"My house is along Sciota Mills Road, which is a county road. There is a Right of Way marker on the exact spot where the county's property ends and mine begins, and that marker also marks the spot where my land ends on the west side, as well as the east edge of von Ranke's property."

"So that is your reference point?"

"Yes. Plus there is a utility pole at the back of my property that is sited on the exact spot where my property ends to the south and the west. If you mark a line from the Right of Way marker on the north end and the utility pole on the south end, you see that the fence is a foot inside my property."

"Have you discussed this with Mr. Ranken?"

"I refuse to have anything to do with that hard headed Kraut. He refuses to see the error of his ways."

"How old is Mr. Ranken?"

"Oh, I suppose he's about my age, give or take a couple years either way."

"So, you've never tried to talk to him about the fence in the last thirty-one years?"

"No, Ma'am. That is what solicitors are for. If you can persuade the Hun to move the fence without having to file suit, then I'll gladly pay your fee. But his kind were always good at gobbling up the land of others. I offer the Sudetenland as a prime example."

Tumbling Blocks

"So you think I ought to have a talk with Mr. Ranken? Maybe that will resolve the issue?"

"Talking never hurts, unless one is another Chamberlain, but it's time for that fence to be removed."

"Well, Mr. Buckle, I will contact Mr. Ranken and see if there is any compromise to be found."

"The only possible solution is for him to tear down that Siegfried Line. I refuse to be part of another Munich—no compromises with those Teutonic troublemakers."

After Buckle leaves her office, Gabby calls Leo Ranken and asks to meet with him. An appointment is set for the next day, and Gabby is to go to the Ranken home for the meeting.

Chapter 30

At ten the next morning Gabby finds the Ranken house. The "Siegfried Line" turns out to be the quintessential picket fence, painted white and running the length of the property between the homes of Ranken and Buckle. Each property is about an acre in size.

Once inside the Ranken home, Gabby is surprised to find Phillip Ranken, son of Leo also there.

"I asked my son to be here since my English is not so good at times," Ranken begins.

"Dad, your English is very good. Miss Gordon, my father is anxious as to the nature of your visit, so he wanted me here."

"I am sorry if my request for a meeting has caused you alarm. I am seeking to resolve a problem before it becomes a legal matter."

"What issue is that?" Phillip puzzles.

"It seems that your neighbor, Mr. Buckle, believes that the fence between your properties is on his land and he wants it removed."

"Is he still beating that dead horse?" Phillip says as he laughs.

"In 1980 Mr. Buckle was ready to file a law suit when his attorney, Nicholas Bresch, disappeared. The files for the suit were recently recovered and now Mr. Buckle wants to proceed."

"Holy cow! I cannot believe Tom is still harboring this." Phillip says in wonder.

"You're on a first name basis with Mr. Buckle?"

"He's my father-in-law."

"Your father-in-law?"

"My wife Anne is his daughter. We grew up here next to each other, went to school together, and became sweethearts in 5th grade. The only glitch in this romantic story is that our fathers have been at each other's throats since we were in diapers."

Tumbling Blocks

"That must make the holidays awkward."

"You have no idea. In order to avoid a diatribe by Tom, we have to pretend that this house does not exist. If we spend Christmas morning here, when we leave to take our kids to Grandpa Tom's we have to get in the car, drive around for ten or more minutes and then arrive back at Tom's house, as if we just left our own house to come to Anne's family home.

"When the children stay at one or the other of their grandparents' homes, like during the summer, they cannot just climb the fence to visit the other."

"*Wie es eigentlich gewesen!*" Ranken shouts as he slams his hand on the arm of his chair.

"Papa, don't get upset."

"What did he say?" Gabby inquires.

"That's his favorite phrase, telling me that he wants me to tell things "as it was.""

"Is there something I missed?" Gabby wonders as she looks back and forth between father and son.

"Dat mad man shoot Wald," Ranken says in a whisper.

"Someone was shot?" is Gabby's startled reply.

"Not a person. Wald was one of dad's favorite Dachshunds. We had two, Wald and Hexl. One day they cornered and killed Sir Francis, a gander that belonged to the Buckles."

"Excuse me, did you say its name was 'Sir Francis'?"

"Yes, for Sir Francis Drake. I know, I groaned when I first heard it way back then. Anyway, Mr. Buckle then shot Wald in anger over it. He claimed that the gander was Anne's pet, though she admitted to me that she hated the darn thing because it was mean and would chase her all the time. That was why my father put up the fence – to keep our dogs off the Buckle's land. All of this trouble stems from that incident."

There is a long silence while everyone seems lost in thought.

"So, vat does all dis mean?" Leo interjects into the silence.

Tumbling Blocks

"Well, Mr. Ranken, it seems that Mr. Buckle's claim is based on the location of the Right of Way marker along the road. He claims that your fence is at least one foot inside his property based on the location of that marker."

"But I had der line checked by surveyor before I put up der fence. I vas careful to place it von foot inside the line laid out by surveyor. Dis makes no sense. Miss Gordon, I vas a tool and die maker all my life, a job that requires very great precision. I know that fence is not on der dummkopf's land."

"Perhaps the surveyor you hired made an error. If that is the case, it would not be your fault that the fence is incorrectly located."

"What do you suggest, Miss Gordon. Does my father need to hire a lawyer?" Phillip asks in frustration.

"I would not do that for now. I would prefer to find a solution that does not involve a legal tug-of-war. Let me see if there is a way to verify the location of the marker."

That afternoon Gabby calls the office of the Stephenson County Highway Department to request that they verify the position of the Right of Way marker in question.

Chapter 31

L ater that same day Sam has just compiled the data from all three computers into one file for safe keeping overnight when Barnes arrives at The Raspitory.

"H, good to see you. How did the first day back at work go?" is Sam's greeting to Barnes.

"It is good to be back doing something useful. I was positively going quite out of my mind rattling around my house."

"So, what brings you here?"

"My dear, I have come to return Colonel Stocker's journal. It was most enlightening. Do you want me to put it back in the file?"

"No, I'll do that. Actually, we've re-arranged everything since you were here last. Let's see where we have that file now." Clicking at her keyboard, she soon announces that the file is still located in the fireproof cabinet. "Well, looks like it's not moved much."

When she opens the file to place the diary inside, Sam is unable to locate H's signed statement that he had borrowed the book.

"Did any of you like remove a note from the 'Stocker Art Donation' file?" Sam asks of all the workers. Blank stares are the only response.

"That's very curious. I placed the statement in there myself," Barnes asserts. "May I see the file?"

"You can look, H, but it's not there."

After turning over every sheet of paper in the file, Barnes has to agree with Sam.

"There's no reason for the note to have been taken out," Sam mutters almost to herself. Since its five minutes to four, Sam tells the workers, "OK, you guys can call it quits for today. See all of you tomorrow."

Barnes starts to comment again on the missing note when Sam throws him a hard glance which says, "Quiet!"

Tumbling Blocks

Once the last worker is out the door, Sam flips open her cell and hits Gabby's number. "We have discovered actually something missing. You better come over here as soon as you can get away." Pause. "OK, see you then."

"What's going on?" Barnes queries as he sits down opposite Sam's work station.

"Don't know. Let's wait for Gabby before we get too far into any speculation." Quicker than Sam would have guessed, Gabby comes through the door.

"Maybe you better lock it so no one walks in on our discussion," Sam suggests.

After locking the door and taking a seat next to Barnes, Gabby asks, "So what gives?"

"You remember how we could like not find anything missing after someone broke in here? Well, we just discovered something."

"What?"

"At the end of the second day of sorting files, you and Glenn had left, but H and I were still here. It was then that H came across the diary of Colonel Stocker in one of the files in the lockable fireproof file cabinet."

"Yes, I wanted to read it, but I was due back to work at the Museum the next day, so I asked to borrow it. At Sam's suggestion, I placed a note in the file where I found it. The note stated that I had borrowed the diary. I signed and dated it and Sam witnessed it."

"Then I forgot to tell you and it wasn't until H brought the diary back this afternoon that we discovered that the note is missing."

"So, what's the significance of the missing note?"

"None of the other workers knows anything about the note. And, we could not find anything missing after the break-in. We all thought it was odd that like someone had spent all that time here, but had taken nothing. Or so we thought."

"I think," Barnes continues, "that whoever attacked the two of us in my office was looking for that diary."

"Are you sure?"

"Whoever assaulted me was looking for something in my office, but we found nothing missing."

"Did you have the diary in a safe or something?" Gabby asks.

"That's the ironic part. It was in the scanner on my desk. I had just finished scanning the last page when I was struck. The intruder probably did not think to check in the scanner. I forgot about it in the aftermath of the attack and those weeks I was off work. Coming across the diary today, I realized that I had neglected to return it, so I brought it in just before four."

"And that's when we found the missing note, or rather realized that the note was like missing, oh, you know what I like mean."

"So," Gabby begins piecing the puzzle together, "you think that our intruder and the one who attacked the two of you are one in the same, and the reason for the museum attack was because the guy knew Doc had the diary?"

"Gotta be," Sam answers, "two assaults, if you count H and me as one, but like nada was missing after someone spent a lotta time digging through files at both locations."

"So, what's so special about the diary?" Gabby asks, her curiosity piqued.

"I read most of it today after I discovered I still had the original. I'll spare you the details of the day-to-day entries through most of the war. There is a lengthy passage about the incident when the Colonel was shot in the leg by an SS officer and then Stocker's seemingly heroic killing of that officer after his gun jammed. Stocker then brags in the diary about taking a Lugar pistol off the dead German before hobbling back to his own lines. Then follow details about his convalescence in a facility in Britain.

"It seems, however, that towards the end of the war Colonel Stocker was returned to active duty and placed in command of a battalion that was assigned occupation duty in a rural part of Austria. While there he stayed in the small town of Unken,

97

where he took for his own use the house of a Colonel Hans Herrmann of the Third Reich."

"Hans Herrmann? Sounds like a character from a B grade movie," Gabby chuckles.

"It does seem too much of a caricature, but that's what the diary reports. Now Hermann had been killed on the Eastern front in 1943 and this was in April 1945 when Stocker takes over the house. Colonel Herrmann's son, also a Wehrmacht officer, had been killed during the Battle of the Bulge in December, 1944. This is what Stocker learned from Herrmann's housekeeper and then recorded in his diary. Probably demoralized after losing her husband and her only child, Frau Herrmann died in January 1945. According to the housekeeper, the Herrmann's had no other relatives, so there were questions about what would eventually happen to the house and its contents.

"Now, here's where it gets interesting. Herrmann had the one and only original print of a photograph by the famous French scientist Étienne-Jules Marey."

"A print of a photograph of a French scientist is valuable?"

"No, my dear. Marey is famous for his photographs of animals and objects in motion. He pioneered and perfected techniques for taking such photographs. I checked on the Internet today and the photographic print which Colonel Stocker took from the Herrmann house is the only known print of that image. Several websites note that the Freeport Art Museum now holds the print. According the Freeport Art Museum's own website, the print was even signed by Marey."

"Ok, so why would anyone care about the diary? The day after the Bresch vault was discovered Amery Stocker asked for the diary, which he suspected was in the Bresch files. I told him that unless there were extenuating circumstances, he would eventually get the diary," Gabby concludes.

"So, he had no reason to go after the diary if he was like going to get it?" Sam asks.

Tumbling Blocks

"I would think so," is Gabby's response.

"Perhaps, what caused him to go after the diary was the fact that I was going to look at it," Barnes wonders aloud.

"But he would not have known that when he broke in here that night, assuming it was Stocker. It was only after the break-in that he, or whoever it was, would have known you were going to read it. And that does not explain why he would risk breaking in here for something he was going to be handed anyway."

"What else was originally in the file with the diary?" Gabby asks as she points to the file cabinet.

"It was a file about the donation of the Marley…"

"Marey, my dear," Barnes corrects.

"…the Marey photo to like the Freeport Art Museum. There was a letter of appraisal for the gift from the Museum director, as well has some forms for an income tax deduction."

"A very large tax deduction if I recall," Barnes adds.

"And what's odd.is that museums and not-for-profits are not allowed to put a value on a gift. The IRS wants independent verification of the value of a donated object if there is a deduction involved, especially such a large deduction."

The trio lapses into silence as each mulls the facts. They are startled out of their reverie by a knock on the door. It's Glenn.

"What are you three up to now that you all look so serious?" he asks after Gabby lets him in and they hug. Due to pressure from his employer because he has taken so much time off work, Glenn has not been back to Freeport for almost a week. The ninety-minute drive each way would have cut into the after hour's work he feels obligated to put in as compensation for his recent long absences.

"We may have a handle on why someone attacked Doc and Sam and broke in here, but all the facts don't add up," Gabby responds.

They retell the sequence of events for Glenn's benefit, but no new conclusions are reached. Finally, Gabby says, "I don't know about you guys, but I'm famished. It's getting too late to go home and fix dinner, so where do you suggest we go?"

"Fast food or more elegant dining?" asks Sam.

"I don't much care one way or the other," Barnes notes.

"Let's make it a quick meal," Glenn suggests.

"Ok, where?"

"H prefers Hyper-burger, but I'm more like a Seedy Bun Place kinda gal," Sam offers.

"Hyper-burger?"

"Oh, that's what I call Burger King because their sandwiches are so big," Barnes chuckles.

"And the Seedy Bun Place?'

"McDonald's because they first began putting sesame seeds on their buns," Barnes explains further.

"Well, regardless of the name, would someone point us in a direction? My stomach's beginning to think my throat has been cut," Gabby grouches.

Chapter 32

B renda Hudson sits at her desk reading emails. In her early sixties, she has been Managing Director of the Freeport Art Museum for over thirty years and is looking forward to soon retiring. At 5' 2" with graying hair dyed to black, too dark given her obvious age, she wears all manner of jewelry. When her phone rings it is the receptionist informing her that her appointment has arrived. Smiling and proffering her hand, she walks over to Barnes as he stands next to the receptionists' desk.

"Good to see you, Dr. Barnes. Won't you come into my office?"

Barnes is always slightly uncomfortable around Hudson. She is too familiar for his taste and seems to believe that all museum directors are part of some secret fraternity.

"What can I do for you today?" Hudson begins as she closes the door to her office.

"I have a question about the Marey print in your collection."

"Oh, that old thing. Why would you be interested in it?"

"I have been reading Colonel Stocker's World War II diary and it has just made me curious to see the print. Is it currently on display?"

"Ahh. No. Unfortunately, it is in storage. As you know, in the museum business we have to keep rotating the collection if we are going to get patrons to return on a regular basis."

"Would it be an inconvenience to have it brought out of storage?"

"Actually, I will have to check, but I believe on second thought that it was sent to a conservator in Chicago for some routine cleaning." She clicks a few keys on her PC and then adds, "Yes, it has been sent out. If you like, I can contact you when it returns."

"That will be fine."

"I did not know that The Colonel kept a diary during the war. Does he mention the Marey?"

"Oh, yes. He describes in great detail where and how he found it."

"We would be very much interested in seeing that diary. It would help us create more of a context for the print. How did the diary come to be in your possession?"

"It was in the files recovered from the Bresch building. I was allowed to look at the diary, which is now in the process of being returned to Amery, Junior, since it rightfully belongs to his family."

"Well, then I'll have to contact Amery to ask permission to also see his father's work."

"Thank you for your time, Ms. Hudson. Good day."

"I'll walk with you to the door."

"I can find my way."

"It's no bother."

As Barnes and Hudson reach the front door, Sam is coming down the ramp to also exit. Sam turns back to the lady who has been escorting her and says, "Thank you for the tour, Miss Shaffer."

Once out in the parking lot, Barnes and Sam get into her Civic and head back to Gabby's office. Unbeknownst to them Hudson sees them get into the same car.

"Any luck?" Barnes asks.

"Yep. It was right there on the wall where you said it would be. It took all my meager will power not to run over and look at it. Instead I continued to feign interest in the other works."

"That no good witch lied to me!" Barnes exclaims. "She said it was not on display and had been sent to Chicago to a conservator for some work. Why would she lie when I could have just as easily walked into that gallery and seen it for myself?"

"Do you think she's working with Amery Stocker?"

Tumbling Blocks

"I'm not convinced that Amery is the culprit in this caper. He's going to get the diary back so why go to so much trouble?"

"Unless there's something in the diary that he doesn't want anyone to see."

"The Amery threat does not explain why Hudson provided so much disinformation on the Marey. She's covering up something, I'm sure."

"Could it be that you just don't like her and therefore you distrust her?"

"That is very possible. The woman is a piece of work. How she manages to keep her job is beyond me. She drinks to excess; I could smell it on her just now and its only 11:00 AM. And all that gaudy jewelry she wears. Every art museum director I've even known is the very model of tasteful dress. This woman looks more like someone who would appear on that Jerry Spritzer Show."

"H, do you mean Jerry Springer? I had no idea you knew about such things."

"As a rule I don't but when one is homebound for weeks on end, there is a limit to how much one can endure before one begins channel surfing."

"I found Anna Shaffer very friendly and competent. Do you suppose we could find a way into the museum's files through her? Might help if we knew what they have on file about the Marey print."

"Couldn't hurt. Do you suppose you could befriend her and gain her confidence?"

"Well, I don't know what sort of relationship she has with her boss. She might not be willing to jeopardize her job for this."

"Perhaps we ought to let Gabby have a chat with her, making it more of a formal request from an attorney working on a case?"

"That's a good idea. If Gabby gets resistance, then we'll know there's no one in the museum we can trust."

Chapter 33

W ith the report from the county highway department in-hand, Gabby arranges a meeting in her office with Ranken, Buckle and their two children.

Everyone is more than cordial with each other when they arrive, except for Buckle and Ranken, who refuse to even look at each other, let alone shake hands.

Gabby begins the meeting by informing all that the location of the Right of Way marker is two feet west of the junction of the three properties—the county's, Buckle's and Ranken's.

"That's impossible," Buckle exclaims. "Did they re-survey the road? I never saw a survey crew."

"They didn't need to, Mr. Buckle. As the county engineer explained to me when roads are built the surveyors drive a one-half inch diameter piece of steel rod into the ground on the exact spot where a property meets the road right of way. The Right of Way marker is placed one foot forward of that steel rod, which is usually a piece of re-bar. When the concrete marker is in place, they then drive the steel rod more than a foot underground to bury it."

"I did not know that," Buckle says in a very quiet voice. "All the county engineer had to do," Gabby continues, "was to locate that original steel marker with a metal detector. He said that the Right of Way marker is two feet west of its underground steel rod. He had no explanation as to why it was mis-located."

"So," Phillip offers, "The fence is properly placed, it's the marker that is in the wrong spot. See, all of this has been a mistake."

"It is not a mistake," Buckle erupts. "I did not come to this country to be fenced in by a dirty Nazi! You Heinie bastards have made my life miserable forever."

"Nien, I vas never a member of the National Socialist Party!" Ranken exclaims as he slams his fist on the table. "And I vas a machinist vorking in a factory during the var. My technical skills made me exempt from military service and I never got involved in politics."

"Then you aided the war effort just the same!" Buckle pronounces. "Dirty Jerrys running riot all over Europe and sending bombers and rockets into London."

"Yah, I vork on making parts of V-1 and V-2 rockets. But ve had no choice. As the var drug on and the Allies ver vinning, many of us in the factory tried to slow production. Some even tried to stop work. Our families vere threatened and some of da men vatched their vives and children shot because dey refuse to vork."

"Should have shot every one of you!" Buckle spits out in bitterness.

Anne puts a hand on top of her father's and tries to calm him. "Dad it's all over now. You've got to let the past go."

As tears begin streaming down his face, Buckle sobs, "But he killed me mum and Annie, me little sister."

The room is silent as all look at Buckle, who makes no effort to hide his tears. In a quiet voice, almost too soft to hear, he continues "They were getting ready for church of a Sunday morning when the sirens sounded. The V-2 rockets arrived so quickly and there was so little time to hide, but it wouldn't have made much difference if they made it to the cellar. Our house took a direct hit. Nothing... left... but... rubble."

"Dad, you never told us," Anne says as she fights back her own tears and puts an arm around her father's shoulder.

"Vat did you do in the var, Mr. Buckle?" Ranken asks in just as soft a voice after a long silence.

A lengthier pause follows while Buckle tries to regain his composure. Finally he speaks, again in almost a whisper. "I was a nose gunner on a bomber. An Avro Lancaster. 106 Squadron. We flew out of Syerston, Nottingham the first half of the war."

"Yah, also too my fadder and mudder vere both killed in a bombing raid," Ranken says softly as if he is in a dream.

Tumbling Blocks

Breaking out of his reverie, Ranken continues, "It is too sad to think of all ve have lost, Mr. Buckle. The var vas not kind to any von. That is vhy I came to America to start over and let the past remain buried with the dead."

No one speaks for several minutes as the younger people try to imagine the hell these two men have experienced, while Leo's and Tom's minds take them back to the horrors of over seventy years ago. Wiping away his tears, Tom breaks the silence.

"Leo, forgive me for being so hurtful. I had no idea of your loss. I have been so consumed with my own grief all these years that I blamed it all on you."

Silence again descends on the room as everyone's heads are bowed, almost as if in prayer. Gabby is about to speak when Buckle clears his throat and then begins a confession.

"The Right of Way marker is in the wrong place. I went out one night after you put in the fence and I dug it up and moved it two feet west just to cause you trouble. In truth, I think the reason I never pursued the law suit when Bresch disappeared was because I knew I was in the wrong. The uncovering of the files brought back all of the hatred I had stored up and repressed for all these years."

Reaching across the table while extending his hand, Buckle says, "Leo, there is no need for you to move or tear down your fence. In fact, if you want my help, I would be honored to help you put a gate in it."

"Yah. That vould be goot. Then our enkelkind can come and go between our houses." The two men shake hands as they stand.

"Miss Gordon," Buckle says as he turns to Gabby "please send me a bill for your services. For the both of us."

"There'll be no need, Mr. Buckle. It was my honor to help bring you two together."

Chapter 34

Joseph Shenk, Jr., shows up at Gabby's office for his appointment twenty minutes early, an appointment to which he has been summoned.

"I took the afternoon off to make sure I was on time," he anxiously tells Gabby after they are in a conference room with the door closed. Sam has joined them.

"You have good news about my grandfather's estate?"

"Well, Mr. Shenk, we have good news and bad news," Gabby begins. "Your grandfather and father were correct. There were some very shady dealings with the estate of Jeremiah Winfrey. In 1971, when Jeremiah Winfrey, Jr. passed away, your grandfather should have split half of at least two million dollars with his three cousins, Cecelia, Geraldine and Alma Winfrey."

"He knew it. Grandpa always said that he was being robbed by that Bresch gang."

"That's the good news. The bad news is that when Nick Bresch disappeared in 1980, so did all of the money in the law firm's operating accounts. He did not touch his firm's trust account, but it now appears that the Winfrey Estate was never included in that trust."

"As near as we can figure," Sam continues, "there was more than two million dollars left in the Winfrey account Nick looted. And that amount does not include the money he took from the joint accounts he had with his wife."

"If they were ripping us off, how come the lawsuits got nowhere?"

"You grandfather and father both hired attorneys from Rockford to file the suits, correct?" Gabby poses. Rockford is the closest large city to Freeport and the county seat of Winnebago County, so there was an abundance of law firms located there for the Bresches to use.

"Yeah. They figured they couldn't trust any attorney here in town to handle the cases."

"And they had to hire attorneys who would not want retainer fees upfront?"

"Yeah, they had no money to pay ahead of time. Thinking on it now, they probably hired poor lawyers."

"They were poor in more ways than one. It looks like the Bresches paid off these lawyers to mishandle the suits. That's why they got dismissed."

"I suspect," Sam adds, "that if those attorney's knew the true value of the Winfrey estate, they would not have been so willing to settle for the small bribes the Bresches handed out."

"So, I'm stuck?" Shenk asks. "I get the moral victory but no cash for me and my wife. And nothing for my distant cousins. Where are they, anyway?"

"We tracked them down in a couple hours. Two, Geraldine and Alma, the twins now live in Dubuque. They're both married, have children and grandchildren."

"Cecilia never married. She lives in Springfield, Illinois where she retired after many years as a clerk for Horace Mann Insurance Company. She's now sixty-nine, but in good health. If you want to get in contact with them, they gave us permission to provide you with their addresses and phone numbers."

"Well, at least I'll get some family out of all this. I'm an only child and so is my wife. Since we have no children, life is pretty lonely with just the two of us. Thank you ladies for your time and efforts. How much do I owe you for your help?"

"There's no charge, Mr. Shenk. Here is a file containing the original copy of Jeremiah Winfrey, Sr.'s Will. We regret that there is nothing we can do at this point to assist you to find the missing money or to initiate some legal action to claim it. If we find anything else, then we'll let you know. Have a good day."

When Gabby returns to her office there is a message for her to call Detective Sumner. The conversation is one-sided, but most gratifying:

"Miss Gordon, I called to let you know that authorities in Conway County, Arkansas have recovered the physical remains

108

of Nicholas I. Bresch, the third, and a Shiloh Deming from an automobile in the bottom of the Arkansas River. Dental records have confirmed the identities. They are also certain that the accident occurred in 1980. Among the personal effects of Bresch was a plastic zip close bag with details of a bank account in the Grand Cayman Islands. I'll FAX over the account number so that you can verify the information. Since there maybe individuals to whom the Bresch law practice owed money, the Chief and I thought that you might like to know all of this. Have a good day."

After hanging up Gabby yells out to Sam, "Get Shenk back here as soon as possible. It's time for Bitter Betty to get some payback."

Chapter 35

T he over-sized chair used by Deacon Root is not occupied so Glenn and Gabby are curious when they're shown into the office of Monsignor Joseph Schwieger, pastor of Saint Martha Parish in Madison. At 5' 1" and over 330 pounds, the Deacon requires a special chair. He owns a small chain of fried chicken restaurants named Herb Chicken, but he has long been his own best customer. He is especially fond of the very crisp flakes of fried coating which accumulate in the bottoms of the deep fryers; hence his impressive girth.

After exchanging pleasantries, Monsignor Schwieger turns to the reasons for the meeting, "I understand that you have questions about Glenn's case before the Marriage Tribunal."

"Yes," Glenn begins. We were under the impression that my case for annulling my marriage to my ex-wife was pretty much a no brainer. Neither of us had ever received a Christian baptism, we were married in a civil ceremony, and since I have now joined the Catholic Church while she has or is about to marry someone else, the case should have gone through with little trouble."

"Now, I am not privy to the Tribunal's deliberations, so I cannot speak to its thinking beyond what they told you."

"The letter informing me of the denial was short and lacked specifics, which is why we are here."

"We called," Gabby adds, "Sister Allison Myers, administrator of the Tribunal. While she was pretty non-committal as to the reasoning for the denial, she did mention that Glenn's petition had been submitted under something called the Petrine Privilege."

"In my meetings with Deacon Herb as he prepared my request, the Petrine Privilege was never mentioned. He kept talking about something called the Pauline Privilege," Glenn notes.
"We'd never heard of it and have done some research on the matter. It seems that Deacon Herb mixed up the Petrine and

Pauline privileges. Pauline Privilege allows for declaring a marriage of two non-baptized individuals to be dissolved if one partner in the marriage later seeks to be baptized and the other doesn't. While I have not read the relevant Canon Law, what we've found makes it clear there was an error in the initial petition."

"Is there an appeal process to the Tribunal or an allowance for error in the original petition that would grant a re-submission of Glenn's request?" Gabby continues.

"If need be, we are willing to retain an outside Canon lawyer to advise us on the case."

"There is an appeal process, but frankly, it could take years. The hiring of a Canon lawyer in such instances could be counterproductive as Tribunals and other Church judicial bodies are very wary of outside parties. The Tribunal process has built into it an adversarial aspect. Deacon Root is pretty insistent that his original submission to the Tribunal was correct. He thinks that the Tribunal was correct in its decision."

"Why isn't he here?" Glenn asks.

"It appears that he feels your personal relationship with him is such that nothing would be gained by such a meeting."

"So, I'm left with little recourse on this because the church official who filed the papers feels some personal hostility to me and I have no reasonable means to bypass him?

"If that's the case, then why didn't he recuse himself from the case when Glenn originally sought to file?" Gabby queries as she begins to become annoyed at what she see as Monsignor's hedging.

"I think it is rather uncharitable to characterize Deacon Root as having any hostility toward you and it is a serious charge to accuse him of deliberately sabotaging your annulment petition," Monsignor replies with an undisguised hint of annoyance. "To what would you ascribe what you perceive as his supposed hostility?"

"Oh, that's a simple explanation. When I attended the final session of the Formation Process after I was Baptized and

Tumbling Blocks

Confirmed, Deacon Root went off on a tirade before the class. In what I can only characterize as a 'melt down,' he told us that since we were now baptized Catholics we are obligated to unquestioningly support, at the risk of committing mortal sin, the Church's teaching on the matter of homosexuality. He railed against homosexuals as if they were the spawn of Satan. I finally interrupted him and asked why the Church was so vehement when it came to not extending the Sacraments to homosexuals, but it is willing to make exceptions for others who are also in clear violation of Biblical teaching. He, of course, asked for an example and I responded 'gluttony'."

Monsignor ponders this revelation for a minute before responding. At length, he says, "Let me make some inquiries, but I cannot promise anything."

On the way back to Freeport, Glenn is pretty glum, a very uncharacteristic mood given his usual upbeat personality.

"I just feel bad for throwing an ecclesial wrench in our wedding plans."

"Don't beat yourself up over this. I would have not been as diplomatic with that old fart if I had been there when he made those comments. We'll work something out."

"I know you've got your heart set on a Catholic wedding, and I am one hundred percent behind that. It's just that I don't really want to wait for however many years an appeal could take."

"Have patience. I know I am not the one who follows that advice for the most part, but with all of the crap happening with the Bresch files, I think we ought to let this ride until we have time to think with clear heads about where to go next. Besides, Monsignor may come up with something. Besides, with any large organization, one person never represents the total. Root, and those of his ilk, are not representative of the total Church. That also means that with any bureaucracy ways can be found around most obstacles created by one individual's pettiness."

Chapter 36

E ven as Gabby and Glenn are coming back from their appointment with Monsignor Schwieger, Betty Bresch drives her car into the parking lot of the Black Hawk War Monument, some sixteen miles west of Freeport. The remote location offers beautiful vistas of the surrounding countryside in addition to marking the site of the graves of members of the Illinois militia who died in the ill-fated efforts by the followers of Black Hawk to resist European-American intrusions on their tribal lands.

Already waiting there in the growing twilight is Brenda Hudson, a woman for whom Betty has little use. But then again, Betty has little use for most other human beings.

A phone call from an unknown man suggested that Bresch and Hudson have mutual interests in keeping hidden certain files that are now in the possession of Gabby Gordon. So Bresch followed his directions to meet Hudson at the site where a young Abraham Lincoln helped bury fellow militiamen in 1832.

Well off the more commonly used county roads, the monument site is popular with area teens seeking a place to party. Because of that, the Stephenson County sheriff's patrols keep a close watch on the place. The presence of two cars there, both driven by women who are obviously well into middle age does not cause concern for the deputy who drives past on routine patrol soon after Betty arrives.

"Glad you got here on time. This place gives me the creeps," Hudson begins.

"What's this all about?"

"There is a file that the bitch Gordon has that I want, and I've been told that she has one you want. So a mutual friend has offered to help." Reaching into her purse Hudson produces a key. "This is to the front door of the store they're using as a temporary office. Use it to gain access one evening and search for our files. But remember that there is a guard there at night from ten p.m. to 6 a.m."

"There could be hundreds of files. It could take hours."

"Use your head—they have to have put them in some alphabetical order. Here's the name on mine." With that Hudson hands Betty a slip of paper.

After looking at the name on the paper Betty says, "What's this gonna cost me?"

"You get your file and mine at the same time."

"What risks are you taking in this venture?"

"As a diversion I'm gonna put some hurt on a certain legal trouble-maker." Hudson's use of the vernacular phrase for attacking someone is at odds with her age, a plethora of homemade jewelry and obvious small stature. But macho talk is something that those who are not particularly brave evidence when trying to talk themselves into taking action. Betty decides to ignore the pathetic bravado of her would be conspirator.

"When?"

"You call to let me know when you're going in and I'll make sure I find her at about that time. My cell number's there on that paper."

"Then what?"

"We'll meet back here twenty-four hours after you get the files. Our friend wants the key back and I get my file."

"Who gave you this key?"

"Don't know. I got an anonymous call. Key then came in the mail. Caller said he'd be in touch when the deed was done."

"This is ridiculous. I prefer to do business with people face to face; knowing all the dogs in the fight."

"That's the deal. Take it or leave it. I can just as easily get inside that office and beat on the minx and you get diddly squat."

"OK. It'll take me a few days to figure out their routine so I can get in without the worry of being discovered. I'll call."

Tumbling Blocks

"If you're smart, you'll get one of those pre-paid cell phones, preferably from some hole-in-the-wall place in Rockford, and then throw it in the river when this show is over."

"This could get expensive."

"How much is that file worth to you?"

Chapter 37

A t the suggestion of Sam and Barnes, Gabby makes a date to have a drink with Anna Shaffer, the curator at the Freeport Art Museum. They met at Eilert's, each having a glass of cabernet.

Miss Shaffer, at 5' 10" was slender, a by-product of marathon running, her favorite pastime. Her soft black, shoulder-length hair and warm dark eyes belied her steely disposition and gritty determination. Both were characteristics which Gabby would come to appreciate.

"I know we met at a fund raiser for the museum a year or so ago, but I was surprised when you called about having a drink after work," Anna begins.

"I'll be honest upfront so that there are no pretenses about why I asked to see you. I am looking to get some information about a piece of artwork in your collection and I've been stonewalled by Hudson. I am hoping that you might help."

"Well, I don't quite know what to say. I certainly do not want to do anything that will jeopardize my job."

"I can appreciate that, and if I begin asking you for information that you feel is too confidential, please tell me. And I definitely need you to keep our talk tonight to yourself, even if you decide you cannot help."

"That is not a problem, unless you are planning something illegal, but then I might be game any way," Anna responds with a twinkle in her eye.

"Trust me, I don't do illegal, at least not if there's a chance I'll get caught. Here's my problem. Among the papers we found in the Bresch Building was a file relating to a photograph donated to the museum by Colonel Stocker."

"The Marey photograph titled 'Tumbling Blocks'."

"Yes, that's it. Last week Dr. Barnes went to see Brenda Hudson to ask to see the photograph. She told him it had been sent out for conservation work and she did not know when it would be back."

"I remember Barnes being at the Museum and the photograph was on display that day. Why would she have told Barnes that?"

"That's part of what we want to know. My secretary, Sam Greer, saw the photograph when you took her on a tour that same morning."

"Oh, yes, the lady with the exquisite tats. So, what is it you want from me?"

"Given Hudson's lie to Barnes, we feel that we need to go around her to examine the museum's file on the photograph. Is that something you can share without breaking too many rules?"

"Ordinarily, I have access to all such files and there has never been anything said about not sharing information with anyone who asks. So, yes, I can get that information without any risks."

"I would urge some precautions in getting that file."

"Really?"

"There's more to the story. In the Bresch law office file about the photograph, there was a diary kept by the Colonel during World War II. In it he describes how he came by the image just as the war ended. The night after we opened the locked file cabinet containing the diary, someone broke into our temporary office, knocked out the guard and went through the files. The only thing missing was a note in the file on the photograph. That note stated that Dr. Barnes had taken the diary to study it. The next evening Barnes was assaulted in his office and then Sam was also assaulted. Near as we can tell the attacker was looking for that diary."

"Wow! That's way weird. So you think that there may be something about the Marey that someone does not want to come to light?"

"That's a good guess. And that someone is willing to hurt people to keep it quiet."

"Do you think its Amery Stocker who's behind this?"

Tumbling Blocks

"We don't think he has a motive. Legally the diary belongs to him and he knows that he'll be getting it soon. So why go to so much trouble?"

"Unless he doesn't want anybody reading it before he gets it."

"But whoever broke into our office did not know ahead of time that Barnes was going to read the diary."

"Hmm. Well, I'll pull our file on the Marey and make a copy of anything I find that seems out of the ordinary. And now that I think of it, when I came in the day after Doctor Barnes was there the Marey photograph had been removed from display and another work was in its place. The removal of any artwork from display without my knowledge is just not done, if for no other reason than those of us who lead tours need to know what's on display so that we can be prepared to answer questions."

"You said 'just not done' in a way that would lead me to believe that you and Hudson do not always agree on things?"

"*Entre nous*, we seldom agree on anything. I feel safe telling you this since we're in this little conspiracy about the Marey, but I just don't know how that woman keeps her job. She drinks heavily, has even come to work in the morning smashed. The average high school art student knows more about art history than she does. I know for a fact that her chief reference for information about artists and artwork is Wikipedia. That's the extent of her research."

"My experiences meeting her have led me to question her artistic tastes given all the gaudy jewelry she wears."

"Oh, she makes her own and calls it art. Most of it wouldn't earn a passing grade in a middle school art class. But we have an exhibit every year of her work, and the museum pays her extra for it. The truth is if I did not know whose jewelry it was, I would not allow the so-called artist to display and sell it at even our annual Art in Park event, let alone exhibit it in the museum."

"She must have someone on your board's support."

118

"That's the bottom line. From what I know, if there is ever a chance for a vote to dismiss her, a certain board member never lets things get to that point."

"Well, Anna, can I get you another glass of wine?"

"Let me buy this time."

"No, this is my treat. I asked for the meeting."

"You know, I feel like one of those characters in a spy movie—snooping around trying to get information and not get caught. A double agent of sorts. How exciting!"

Chapter 38

Armed with the information in the Winfrey Estate files, Gabby realizes that sans some intervention by a court, the money Nick Bresch stashed in the account in the Grand Caymans will go to Bitter Betty. As a result Gabby gets Joe Shenk's hearty consent to begin legal proceedings. Weighing her options, Gabby decides to confront Betty Bresch before actually filing the suit. The goal of the meeting is to get Bresch to agree to a settlement before anything becomes public.

Reluctantly, but perhaps with hopes that the Bresch law practice files are going to come to her, Betty agrees to the meeting with Gabby. At the outset, Gabby tells Betty that the meeting is being tape recorded.

"Listen, bitch, you can bring in a boatload of stenographers if you want, it won't change anything I have to say. So why have you bothered me? Decided to just give me the files?"

"Weston and Sanderson has been approached by an individual who has legal claim to the Winfrey Estate."

"That old dog jumped the fence years ago. And why would that involve me?"

"We have uncovered conclusive proof that for many, many years your husband and his father schemed to deprive the Winfrey descendants of their fair share of the estate."

"Well, both of the bastards are dead. You gonna dig 'em up and put their bones on trial? Then pull the gold from their teeth to pay off the settlement?"

"That won't be necessary. You see the Bresch law firm had sole control of the Winfrey Estate, including all of the money. So all my client will seek is a return of what is rightfully his."

"You dimwit! That lousy jerk known as my husband looted all the accounts before driving off with that mini-skirted pissant. There is no money, and I've got a lawyer who'll argue that my assets are not subject to such a suit. I've won that one before."

"But what about all the money on Grand Cayman?"

"How'd you find…I mean…what account in Cayman?"

"The one your late husband set-up before leaving and for which he was carrying the account number when he died?"

"I-I-I-I…I know nothing about such an account, you liar," Betty hisses.

"I am sure that an audit of the activity of the account will show that transactions for that account will correspond with bank records here for removal of funds all those years ago."

"You're a liar. That money is mine. Pain and suffering justify my getting it, all of it. I'll fight you in the street outside the courthouse if I have to. You'll never lay a finger on any of it!"

Bresch is on her feet, leaning in across Gabby's desk, spittle spewing with every word she snarls. Gabby sits back calmly, fully intending not to be drawn into a shouting match in this return bout.

"You blood sucking lawyers are all alike. They must give you some sort of vaccine in law school to make you such loathsome creatures. Nick's dad was just like you, not a thread of kindness in him anywhere. He constantly berated Nick for being generous. The Bresches were all alike—grab as much as you can.

"Well, I'll tell you something you meaningless dog turd, I intend to grab all I can get—they taught me real good, and I'm not going to let anyone, especially a minx just out of law school, take what is mine."

"You do understand, Ms. Bresch, that once this suit is filed and it becomes known publicly that the overseas account exists, then anyone else who was owed money by your late husband's law firm will probably also file?"

"Bring 'em on. I'll move someplace where no one can touch me or the money if I have to. This stink hole has no hold on me. I might even just abandon my house and let you and the rest of the starving pack fight over that bone. Yeah, that's it. Pit all you bitches against one another. See who'll be the last dog standing after that fight."

"If we can settle this without filing a suit, then you have a better shot at keeping the existence of the Grand Cayman account secret."

"As if that's gonna happen. As soon as I settle with you, you'll begin sniffing around for anyone else who has some petty claim on Nick's business. I caught scent of you coming a mile away. That mangy dog stink you give off would make a dead man gag. Go ahead and file your suit. It will be the last one you'll ever file!"

With that Betty is heading for the front door of the law offices. Gabby could see that all of the voles in the office are peering from behind various objects just to get a glimpse of the infamous Bitter Betty.

As Gabby shuts off the tape recorder on her desk, Sam comes in, closing the door behind her.

"Well," Sam snorts, "I could have taken all of her statements down from my desk out there. The woman has lungs."

"Unfortunately for her, she has little or no sense. She admitted two things that will bolster our case: one, that she knew that the off-shore account exists; and two, that she's willing to flee U.S. jurisdiction in order to keep the money. The critical thing will be to get the suit filed and then a court order to keep her from leaving the country. She gave us grounds for such an order and we better get one before she can pack-up. I'll need you to type up, as soon as you can, a transcript of my meeting with Bitter Betty to use in support of our case."

"All of the Winfrey files are in The Raspitory. How do you want to proceed?"

"I'll go over after work this evening and begin to outline the case. Glenn has some client he's taking to dinner tonight in Madison, so I'll be free to work."

Tumbling Blocks

"You want me to come over?"

"No, go home and have a quiet evening. You've put in way too many long hours in the past few weeks."

"You're the boss. Want me to bring you something to eat later?"

"Thanks, but no. I'll need to take a break at some point, so I'll probably wonder over to Union Dairy for a brat."

Chapter 39

Afront of unseasonably cool air for July has settled over Freeport, so Gabby wishes she'd taken a jacket with her as she heads back to The Raspitory from Union Dairy shortly after 8:30 that evening. As she steps into the alley along Van Buren between Stephenson and Main, a heavy, blunt object catches her behind the ear. Instinctively turning toward the sudden pain, she gets a glimpse of an arm holding a pipe or a …

In a reflex of self-preservation, her conscious mind shuts down in response to the sudden, overwhelming pain. Later she will recall a feeling of drifting in darkness with no sense of up or down, back or front.

"It must not have been my time to go, because I saw no white light and there was no one beckoning me to walk toward it," she later jokes.

When Gabby regains consciousness she is in an ambulance on the way to the hospital. An EMT with "Jay" on his name badge is asking her questions. Irritated with what she feels are stupid questions she demands her purse and cell phone.

"Sorry, ma'am, we did not find them at the scene."

"Well, shit and shoved in it!"

"Beg your pardon, ma'am?"

"You gotta radio the police and tell 'em to get over to my office, someone probably took my stuff to get the keys."

"When we get to the hospital, I'll inform the officers."

"Listen…'Jay'…call them now! I am not the first person to be assaulted over access to my office in the past few weeks. This is important." With that, Gabby lets go of the EMT's shirt and collapses back on the stretcher, a wave of nausea sweeping over her.

Responding to a radio message relayed from the EMT the officers still at the scene of the attack run down the block and around the corner in time to see a woman with her arms full of files leaving The Raspitory. Within minutes they arrest Betty Bresch.

Chapter 40

"We recovered four pretty big files that the perp was trying to take from your office," Detective Sumner tells Gabby as she lay in a hospital bed the next morning.

"Bet they all had "Winfrey" on them."

"The three biggest did, but one had 'Stocker' on it."

"Really?"

"The perp insists that that file was picked up by mistake. All she wanted were the files which belonged to her now deceased husband."

"Bull roar! She's trying to block people with legal claims to money her husband tucked away in that off shore account. I strongly suggest that if she manages to post bail then the judge should confiscate her passport and require she remain within the city."

"I'll pass that on. Any other details you can recall?"

"Just blackness and then lots of pain and then more pain followed by even more pain."

"Just so you are aware, those files are now evidence and you may not see them for some time if she fights this."

"Not a problem. We photocopied all of the files we figured might be targets, so we have the originals. What she got were copies."

"Smart move."

"I assume you recovered my purse and cell?"

"Yes. In a trash can about a block away from where you were mugged."

"Which way?"

"At the east end of the alley."

"That makes no sense. Why would someone clobber me to get the keys to my office but then head away from the office? Was I hit that hard?"

"Well, we were wondering the same thing. Your office keys were in your purse, while the key we found on Mrs. Bresch was not on any key ring. Did you have an extra key on you?"

"No, just the one on my key chain, which also has my car and house keys on it. All those keys were there?"

"Mr. Logan and Miss Greer IDed them, along with your purse and cell. You see, what we can't figure is why you were hit. There was a man jogging down Stephenson who saw you go down and he came immediately to you. He called nine-one-one on his cell as he saw the perp dump your purse in a trash bin where the alley opens onto Chicago Avenue."

"Who was this Good Samaritan?"

"Tim Rinker, a teacher at Freeport High School. Most people in town call him 'Forest' for the character Forest Gump because he is always running in and around the city; competes in marathons and such."

"I'll have to remember to send him a thank you note. So there would have not been time for Betty to hit me, dump my purse, walk back the block and a half to the office, unlock the door, look for files and still be there when your officers arrived?"

"That's just what has us puzzled. Did the person who hit you do it so Mrs. Bresch could get in without your returning too soon, but Mr. Rinker's untimely arrival messed it up, or…"

"Was I hit by someone who wanted my purse and keys but was not involved in Betty's pilfering?"

"Precisely. Bresch had her own key. So far she's refused to admit to even having an accomplice, though it's hard to believe she wasn't involved in your mugging since she seems delighted to hear that you were hurt."

"In case you've not noticed, Betty Bresch has little sympathy for anyone but Betty. I sometimes think she'd run down her own grandmother if there was profit in it."

"Having questioned her for several hours, I have to agree. Now, just to save me and the DA a lot of time digging, what did she want with those files?"

Tumbling Blocks

"Her husband's law firm had been siphoning off money from the Winfrey estate for decades. We found the proof when we examined the law firm's older accounts. A descendant of Winfrey is ready to file a suit in an effort to recover funds from the account on Grand Cayman. I believe that she wanted to destroy any evidence of fraud since she knew about both the off-shore account, as well as from where the money in that off-shore account came."

Chapter 41

Home from the hospital a day later, Gabby is ensconced on a couch in Babcook Manor's family room with Glenn, Sam and Sarah there to shepherd her convalescences.

"Doctor's orders," Sarah is saying, "You must stay off your feet for a couple days. Concussions are nothing to fool with." Sarah is using her best Physician's Assistant voice, a mixture of stern and comforting, to keep Gabby from heading back to work or engaging in her usual very physical activities.

"H and I had to like take it easy for a while so you're no different," Sam scolds.

"Well, I feel fine and the lump is going down. It grates me to have to just sit here and stare at the walls."

"Like why don't ya use the time to watch those DVDs of "NCIS" you got for Christmas? Then you and Glenn will have something actually in common."

The silence with which this statement is met causes Sam to re-run it in her head.

"Well, what I meant like was that he's actually like quoting from the show and none of us ever watch it, so it'd be like cool if at least one of us actually knew what he's talking about, like. Guys, come on here, help me. Glenn, you know what I meant, right?"

"Sam, you're just digging a deeper hole and we're all having fun watching you. We know what you meant, no one is offended, so just let it go," Glenn finally chimes in to relieve Sam's discomfort.

"If the doctor's orders allow and Nurse Ratchet here is OK with it, can I at least think and talk?" Gabby pleads mockingly.

"As long as you don't overdo it and remain seated with your feet up, I think I can keep from having to perform a frontal lobotomy," Sarah responds with a terse smile.

Tumbling Blocks

"So, let's try to figure out what happened last night. Whoever slugged me and took my purse was not Bitter Betty, since it appears as though she was already inside the office when I was whacked," Gabby begins.

"But who else has a motive?" Glenn follows.

"And how did Bitter Betty get a key?" Sam puzzles.

"That's a good place to start. It could be that the person who took my purse had nothing to do with Bitter Betty's busted break-in," Gabby responds.

"Hey," Glenn exclaims, "alliteration is probably a violation of doctor's orders. Right, Sarah?"

"Could your mugging have been set-up in case you came back to the office too soon?" Sarah queries, ignoring Glenn's comment.

"Detective Sumner suggested something along that line. But it is also possible that the timely arrival of this Tim Rinker guy forced the thief to ditch my purse prematurely."

"That would point to the two events being unrelated, just a coincidence," Glenn speculates. "But Gibbs' rule number thirty-nine states there's no such thing as a coincidence."

"There you go again," Sam moans.

"It's OK, Sam," Gabby says. "I don't mind as long as he doesn't start calling me Addie."

"It's Abby and you'd be more like a Ziva," Glenn responds.

"As I said, 'I don't mind.' But leaving the mugging aside for now, how did Bitter Betty get a key?"

"There is always the possibility that some previous tenant of the building had some contact with her and she acquired a key that way," Glenn muses.

"Sam, tomorrow why don't you contact the owner of the building to determine when the locks were changed last and if more than one tenant before us used the same keys, then we'll try to find a link to Bitter Betty," Gabby states.

"Are there other people who have exhibited any extraordinary interest in the contents of those files?" Sarah poses.

"Not really. Like we've been getting calls at the office all along and some people have called numerous times, but no one seems to have been like overly anxious. But I will actually check with all of the guys at the office who answer calls to see if anyone has noticed any patterns," Sam concludes.

"What files did Betty have on her?"

"Three Winfrey and one Stocker. But Sumner said that she claims that she grabbed the Stocker file by mistake," is Gabby's response.

"Is that possible? Were all those files in close proximity to each other?" Glenn puzzles.

"Come to think of it, no they weren't. We assumed that whoever had been hitting people over the head was after the Winfrey file, so the duplicates were intentionally left lying out on a desk in an effort to make sure that whoever came in would not trash the place looking for them," Gabby offers.

Interrupting, Sam continues, "That's right. Actually the Stocker file was on my desk all the way on the other side of the room. That file was there because I had like just finished making a copy at the law office, which is where I left the original in the safe."

"So," Glenn reasons, "If Bitter Betty had that file she must have gone looking for it. And it was no accident that she had it, unlike what she told the cops."

"But why would she want that file? Her problems are tied to the Winfrey estate."

"Ah, my head is spinning," Gabby whispers.

"That's it, everyone out. Gabby, you stretch out and close your eyes. Glenn, before you go, please lower the blinds to darken the room." Sarah is up and in charge as everyone scatters to create some quiet for Gabby.

Three hours later, groggy from a long nap Gabby pads into the kitchen in search of something to eat. She comes across Sarah and Alys sitting at the island talking quietly over cups of coffee.

"Hey, girl, what ya doing up and around?" Alys begins.

"Got the munchies. Thought I'd try to conjure up an apple," Gabby responds as she reaches down to rub Irish Red's ears as he rises to greet her.

"Go back and lie down, we'll get it for you," Sarah orders as she heads for the refrigerator and Alys jumps up to escort Gabby back to the family room.

"You guys make me feel like an invalid. I can still walk and talk and even eat ice cream all on my own. Feels like you'll be bringing in tour groups soon to observe 'the wounded attorney in her natural habitat'."

"Not the right time for us to exert our independence genes," comes Alys' reply. "Sarah is not very patient with patients who disobey her orders and we would not want to get crossways with a medical professional, now would we?"

"When did 'we' develop the third person 'we'?" Gabby asks as she sits back down in a recliner.

"Comes from living with a nurse for many years. Medical situations always bring out that side of 'us'."

"Here we are," Sarah chirps cheerfully as she enters the room. "Cored and sliced."

"Is it against doctor's orders for me to eat an apple whole?"

"Don't get testy. Just trying to make things a little easier," Sarah mildly scolds.

"Sorry, I guess I am not a very good patient and have never taken to being babied. I do appreciate your being here and all the expert care."

"Spoken like a truly chastised and repentant invalid."

"Just to bring you up to date," Alys begins in an effort to change the subject, "I installed that video surveillance system we discussed. I hid as best I could the four cameras that came with the system, they are positioned so that anyone inside the workspace can be seen from multiple directions. It will not be able to record if anyone is trying to break it, but once inside the office, they will be caught from enough angles that we should be able to ID them."

Tumbling Blocks

"Thanks for doing that, Alys. I hate to spend the money to have an alarm system installed in what is a temporary office, so that off-the-shelf system you found ought to work. Maybe we'll get lucky and nail whoever is messing with us," Gabby says with enough edge in her voice that Sarah is about to speak, but Gabby quickly adds, "I know, I'll calm down. See, just as relaxed as Alfred Thayer laying on the carpet in a pool of sunlight on a winter's afternoon."

"Except for that vein sticking out of your neck," Alys notes.

"So, rat me out? Well, what do you want? Someone's messing with people who mean something to me, not to mention messing with me, too, and I'm getting pretty pissed off."

"I know, Gabby, but getting upset right now is only going to prolong your being confined to bed rest. So let it go for now and concentrate on relaxing. Is there something we could put on TV that would help?"

"I guess you're right," Gabby concedes as Irish Red sits down next to her and she reaches down to again rub his ears. "Oh, yes, Mom and Dad got me a DVD set of *The New Yankee Workshop*. Maybe that will keep my interest. I've never watched it, but Dad highly recommended it. Of course, this is from a guy who thinks that *How It's Made* is award winning television."

"I love *The New Yankee Workshop*," Alys squeals with delight.

"OK, girl, you're on. We'll watch whatever they do on the show for the rest of the afternoon."

"Gotta love that woodshop Norm has. Someone once observed that he never changes router bits, he just changes routers."

"My kinda guy," Gabby adds as she and Alys high-five.

"You two are a real matched set. As long as you don't end up out in the garage trying to build something, watching TV for a few hours should be relaxing," Sarah pronounces in granting her imprimatur to the plan.

Glenn arrives back at Babcook Manor just as Gabby and Alys finish the second disk of the set.

"Sarah, have you checked Gabby's vitals lately?" he asks as he walks into the family room.

"No, is there a problem?"

"You actually got Gabby to watch TV? Something's wrong, way wrong. Maybe she ought to have an MRI or Cat-Scan or something."

"Don't be sarcastic, mister. Alys and I have been having fun watching Norm. I have compiled a list of tools and equipment I want for my shop. Of course, we'll need to add on at least fifty percent more square footage to the garage in order to house all of it."

"I told your dad that buying that set would lead to trouble, but he insisted that you would appreciate the quality of the workmanship."

"Adding on to the back of the garage would be a cinch. Want me to develop some plans?" Alys offers.

"You go, girl. Let's think state-of-the-art. Make ole Norm's plaid shirts turn green with envy," Gabby adds with glee.

"I can't believe this. Sarah, isn't this against some order from the doctor?"

"Hey, Glenn, she's sitting, not fighting me about wanting to get up to go re-hang the garage doors, so let them be."

Chapter 42

After a few days spent recuperating under the watchful eyes of Alys and Sarah, Gabby is finally deemed well enough to be left alone during the day, doctor's orders still requiring her to refrain from strenuous activity. Having finished all the DVDs of *The New Yankee Workshop,* Gabby turned to a set of DVDs of *This Old House* which Alys loaned her. In the middle of one episode she becomes aware of movement out of the corner of her eye. Not wanting to call attention to her position, she slowly turns to look out a window to the back lawn of Babcook Manor. There she sees a man walking around as if he is inspecting the trees.

Gabby is about to dial 911 when she recognizes something about the way the man walks. Then she realizes who it is—Tom Reining, her ex-husband.

"What brings you back here?" she queries as she opens the sliding glass door onto the patio.

"Oh, Gabby, you scared me," Tom answers. "I had no idea you'd still be living here. I just stopped to see how the rehab job turned out."

"So you're checking up on my work?"

"I guess, kinda."

"Drove all the way here from wherever just to see what I did with the place?"

"Actually, from Janesville, but no, not just to check up on your work." Tom stands there with his head hanging down for almost a minute before he speaks again. "I need your help. Can we talk?"

"Have a seat here on the patio," Gabby gestures as she closes the door after allowing Irish Red to come outside with her.

The dog goes to Tom, checks him out but does not offer her usual wagging tale. *He must sense my being unsettled* Gabby thinks to herself.

Tumbling Blocks

"So, what gives?" she begins as she takes a seat opposite a man she has not seen or heard from in over four years. Irish Red sits next to her, facing Tom, his ears up in the alert position.

"You may not know that when I left Freeport I got a job with a law firm in Cleveland where David Trask worked. You remember him? My buddy from law school."

"Yes, he was best man at our wedding."

"Oh, yeah, that's right. Ha-ha, forgot about that. Well, anyway, as you know, I have a habit of getting myself into jams, and I managed to do so again. I married a woman…"

"Let me guess, you handled her divorce and she's very young?"

"You know me too well. She's twenty now, but she found out that I've not been exactly faithful, so she divorced me."

"And you weren't smart enough to get a pre-nuptial agreement and she's taken everything?"

"I'm beginning to feel you've been writing the script of my life."

"So, you need money to pay off the settlement?"

"No, I had to get my dad to pay out my share of his construction company to pay her off. Basically, she took my inheritance. And then the law firm fired me."

"Have you been able to get into another firm?"

"No. My track record is too screwed up for anyone to take me on."

"So, you need money to set-up your own practice?"

"No, I'm finished with the law."

"Had your law license pulled?"

"Yep."

"How are you living?"

"I've gone to work for my dad's company. The prodigal son may have had the fatted calf served up, but the best I could do was get hired as one of my dad's hourly workers. My two brothers are not happy about the situation. They figure it'll only

135

be a matter of time before I con dad into giving my share of the business back and thereby reducing their ultimate shares."

"So, why are you here?"

Tom takes his time answering, fixing his eyes on the patio at his feet. It is as if he is wrestling with having to confess his sins in public. At length he starts, "I got mixed up with a loan shark while I was in transition between Cleveland and home. Now that I'm working for Dad I've got income but not enough to cover in one payment the money I owe the shark. I'm into them for twenty-thousand plus the vig."

"Plus the what?"

"Vig. That's street slang for the interest on money owed a loan shark."

"So, how much do you owe, counting the vig?"

"Pretty close to thirty grand."

"And you think I'm good for it? After you kicked me in the gut and left me with this place?"

"Well, I was hoping you'd sold the place by now and that you'd cleared enough to let me have something for old time's sake."

"You're not helping your sales pitch here by bringing in our past soured relationship. Besides, by the time I finished this place I had so many loans outstanding I couldn't sell it for enough to begin to break even. You do know that the housing market tanked in oh eight?"

"Yeah. I guess I was hoping against reason that you had come out ahead on the house and that you could let bygones be bygones. I honestly had no idea you'd be living here. I just stopped by to look the place over. You did a fantastic job, by the way."

"With no thanks to you for leaving me in such a mess."

"Well, I guess I wasted a day off and the cost of the gas to come out here."

Gabby does not answer. After a long silence Tom gets up to leave.

Tumbling Blocks

"Where are you living?" she asks as he reaches the edge of the driveway.

"I got an apartment there in Janesville."

"Give me your address and I'll see what I can do. No promises."

"Gabby, anything, anything you can do will be great. I'll put my address on the back of my company's, well, Dad's company business card."

When he hands Gabby the card, she snaps it out of his hand as she levels her eyes and says, "This is it for us. If I send you something, and that is still a very big 'if,' the debt you'll owe me is that you never, ever come back into my life. Is that understood?"

"Yes. I get it. You'll never see or hear from me again, irregardless of what you decide. I'm grateful that you're even considering it."

Gabby then turns and goes back into the house, not watching as Tom walks down the long drive to his car, which is parked out on River Road. Irish Red stands guard by the door until Tom is out of sight, then the dog trots to the living room window to watch Tom until he gets in his car and leaves.

Chapter 43

S itting back on the couch in her family room Gabby wrestles with what to do. She fears that bailing Tom out will only make her an enabler and further his bad habits. Yet she is aware that while finishing the house had been three long years of hard work and a financial strain, the settlement from Galway's Will left her way ahead of where she would have been by simply selling the place.

The real question with which she wrestles about helping Tom is whether or not her help will insure that she never hears from him again, or will it just encourage him to come back again and again. Her ability to be hard edged when it comes to advocating for her clients is not generally reflective of her basic personality. She is often inclined to help the downtrodden, so her own financial status inclines her toward granting Tom's request.

Five minutes later she is on a ladder pushing the access panel open to the attic space of the house. Armed with a flash light and a plastic bag, she works her way across the joists to the opening into the conical attic space above the turret. One of the biggest features of Babcook Manor's French Norman style architecture is the turret.
Being back in the attic space reminds her of the time she and Glenn searched for money that was supposed to be hidden in the house. Finding the money and determining that it was probably blood money from Galway's "hits," they have left it hidden. Now she lifts away the panel that covers the small opening into the turret's attic and in doing so she's hit with a blast of very hot air.

I need to get some sort of ventilation in this space. Its way too hot in here, she thinks as she crawls inside. There she finds, just as she and Glenn left them over two years ago, 56 brick-size bundles. Each bundle, wrapped in visqueen plastic, consists of a mixture of hundreds and fifties--$10,000 in each bundle. She puts three of the bundles in her plastic bag. As she nears the opening back to the main attic the heat overcomes her and she begins to feel weak and dizzy.

Oh, crap. I guess this was not such a good idea.

The relatively cooler air of the better ventilated general attic space beckons and she wills herself to continue to move. Once out of the turret's oppressive heat she sits for a few minutes trying to catch her breath and regain her senses. The smells of the long enclosed attic waft into her consciousness. After moving the cover back over the turret opening, she carefully stands, not sure if the dizzy spell has passed. As she begins to feel her balance is up to the task, she gingerly walks across the joists to the hatch that opens down into the closet of the master bedroom.

Gabby is closing the access panel to the attic when she hears a voice from downstairs.

"Gabby, where are you?" Alys calls from the bottom of the stairs.

Stuffing the plastic bag and flash light into a corner of the walk-in closet, she quickly folds the step ladder and sets it in another corner. Walking out into the air conditioned space of the master bedroom, Gabby is just barely able to close the closet door before she collapses. It's only a matter of minutes before Alys finds her. Just as Alys is about to dial 911 on her cell, Gabby regains consciousness and calls for Alys to stop.

'Good God, woman. Look at you, you're soaking wet with sweat. You need to go to the hospital. This is not good."

"It's OK. Please Alys, don't make this into something it's not. I tried to use the treadmill and when I realized that I was overdoing it, I headed up here to get a shower. I must have passed out for a second. Lesson learned. No exertion for a few more days."

"Let me help you to the bed," Alys comforts as she lifts a protesting Gabby and carries her to the bed.

"Just get me a glass of water and give me a minute. I was not out long because I remember hearing you call my name. I'll be OK. And please don't tell Sarah about what happened."

Tumbling Blocks

"As if that's gonna happen. She'll be home soon and you have to let her check you out. That's not negotiable."

After almost an hour of checking and rechecking heart rate, blood pressure and numerous other vital signs, Sarah is finally convinced that Gabby's OK and that the incident need not be mentioned to Glenn on the condition that Alys will babysit Gabby for a couple more days.

The next morning, while Alys is outside giving Irish Red his daily grooming, Gabby conjures up a box, puts the three bundles of cash inside, tapes it shut and puts Tom's address on it. Later she asks Alys to take the package to the Post Office during a trip into town to run errands.

Chapter 44

A week later Gabby is still getting back on her feet from the restrictions the doctor imposed. Under orders to take slow paced walks each day, she decides to spend time wondering around Farm and Fleet. While looking at power tools that would be great to have in her newly planned workshop she sees Anna Shaffer coming towards her.

"Hi, Anna. You are on my list of people to call."

Anna whispers, "Please don't call me, especially at work. I can't explain now. I need to talk to you, but I am sure I'm being followed all the time. So, just listen. Each night about five I go for a run. Some evenings I run through Krape Park. Tomorrow at about seven forty-five meet me on the Yellow Creek Nature Trail. Take the left fork after the entrance and then wait at the second bench on the left. If I run by and do not stop, it means that I'm being followed and will try to double back. If you can't make it tomorrow, then we'll try for the day after." In a louder voice, Anna concludes, "Well, great seeing you Gabby," and walks off.

The puzzling encounter with Anna is racing around Gabby's mind as she drives back to Babcook Manor. Sitting at the stop light at the intersection of Lincoln and West, she realizes that in the car next to her is Joe Blunt. Horror crosses Gabby's face when she notices that he's picking his nose while waiting for the light to change. Not just picking it, but digging in with real gusto.

Gabby looks away just as Joe turns his head to look in her direction. Pretending to adjust the radio, a honk of the horn of the car behind her reminds her that she can turn right on red, relieving her of the risk of having to face the obnoxious real estate broker.

Gabby will never know that the turn of her head will be interpreted by Joe as her being angry with him; his absent-minded proboscis probing not-with-standing. He comes to

141

believe that Gabby is angry over his part in having brokered the deal when she and Glenn purchased the Bresch Building. Joe, despite his bravado of self-promotion, possesses an ego that is as fragile as a cheap crystal vase.

That same afternoon at a Chamber of Commerce Business After Hours event held at Citizens State Bank, Joe sees Gabby across the room. He has already been at a bar for an hour before the event, and is now on his second glass of wine at this gathering. Fortified with the false courage of wine he goes to Gabby intent on reaffirming their friendship.

"Just wanted to let you know that I feel badly about the Bresch thing and that I will handle the sale of the vacant lot for no fee just to show there are no hard feelings," he stammers as he offers a handshake.

Well aware that common knowledge around town holds that Joe never washes his hands after going to the bathroom, Gabby pretends to juggle her cup of coffee and plate of snacks. Without looking up, Gabby says, "Well, Joe, we've not yet decided on selling, but if we do, we'll give you every consideration."

Gabby's non-committal response leads Joe's fragile ego to throw his mind out of gear, so he mindlessly plunges into a topic he is supposed to avoid. "Oh, by the way, I hope you're not mad about me loaning my key to the old Freeport Hardware Store."

Gabby's sudden head turn at that comment makes Joe realize that he has crossed a line that was not to be crossed.

"Well," he stammers as he wipes the palm of his hand on his rotund belly, "I gotta go. Always things to do in the real estate business. Remember, 'if it's a house you want, just call Joe Blunt.' With that he is rushing out the door before she can respond.

Chapter 45

An hour later Glenn, Gabby and Alys are discussing the proposed rendezvous with Anna.

"There is no way I am going to let you go out on that trail alone after what happened just a couple weeks ago," Glenn says in as forceful a voice as Gabby has ever heard him use.

"I won't be doing anything but sitting on a bench. If Anna comes by and she's not being followed, then we will talk. Otherwise I'll just come home."

"I do not like it one bit. What if whoever is following Anna recognizes you and decides to finish what he started?"

"Or, what if Anna is part of the conspiracy?" Alys chimes in. "This is not a good idea. How many folks have to get hurt over this whole thing?"

"Look, it's a public park with an hour of good sunlight left. It's not some dark alley. Besides, I trust Anna," retorts Gabby.

"Please rethink this," Glenn begs, his demanding tone having already succumbed to Gabby's generally unbending will.

"I can't call Anna, so how are we supposed to talk? She must have something important to tell me or she wouldn't go to such lengths."

"Like Alys says, maybe she is working with whoever is behind all of this. It could all be a set-up to get you alone."

"I doubt that, she just doesn't seem like the type. I'm going and that's the end of it. But I will take Irish Red with me, just to ease your mind."

"Oh, sure, take along a dog as protection, but this dog would lick you to death before he'd consider even growling," Alys answers.

"Those are my terms," Gabby concludes as she walks out of the room.

As Gabby leaves, Alys and Glenn look at each other with eyebrows raised and then knowingly nod.

Chapter 46

Parking her car several hundred yards from the entrance, Gabby's walk to the trail head is interrupted by a very elderly man who is shuffling along the edge of the road in a geriatric version of jogging. When she notices that he is trying to make eye contact with her, Gabby feigns an interest in Yellow Creek as she crosses the bridge. Her efforts are to no avail as the man stops when he is next to her on the bridge.

"Say, aren't you that missy who was in the paper awhile back about some tough guys from Chicago?"

"Yes," is Gabby's curt reply.

"You know, I figure a smart gal like you would be on to them."

"Who?"

Leaning closer, he whispers, "The Canucks."

"The what?"

"You know, the Canucks. The Canadians. Our supposed neighbors to the north."

"What about the Canadians?"

"Don't you see? Or maybe you're trying not to admit the truth when it's staring you right in the face."

"What truth?"

"Them. They're taking over our country."

"Who?"

"The Canucks."

"Why?"

"We got all the warm weather. They want Florida and California. Arizona, too. Heat. When you have a land frozen in ice, Tampa and Phoenix look very inviting."

"But they can go to those places whenever they want."

"So it seems," the old man said as he rose on his toes and pointed an index finger at Gabby in a swooping, upward motion. "But the exchange rate is killing them. If they occupy the U.S., then they can control the exchange rate."

"And how are they doing this?"

"Taking over?"

"Yes. Are they going to send their army down here?"

"Oh no. The Canadians are too smart for that. They are very subtle and pretend to have a peaceful nature that is like a sheep's clothing on a wolf."

"Oh?"

"Yeah. Going way, way back, they have been infiltrating our culture so that we won't object when they stage their final coup. Icons of American TV have been subtly fomenting their propaganda for decades. Raymond Burr, Loren Greene and even that icon of American Indians—Jay Silverheels."

"Really?"

"Bet you never knew they were all Canucks. And those pop singers like Céline Dion and Justice Bieber. And then there are the comedians. Very subtle, like white ink on white paper. Get us laughing at their jokes so we don't notice what they're up to. Jim Carrey, Mike Myers and Dan Aykroyd. All Canucks."

"Sir, I've got to go. And I think you've been watching too many programs about conspiracy theories," Gabby says as she starts to walk away.

"But you need to listen. The clincher, the one that proves my case is Alex Trebek on 'Jeopardy.' He's a Canuck. Ever notice how many categories and questions deal with Canada?"

At this point Gabby becomes aware of the sound of car tires on gravel behind her. A Freeport Park District Police car slowly rolls to a stop beside the old man. Through an open window, the officer says, "OK, Rick. Time to move on. The bus is waiting for you at the top of the hill."

As the old man moves off, the officer says to Gabby, "Retired insurance adjustor who has gone round the bend. The nursing home where he lives brings him here in the evenings to walk, but mainly to get him away from the other residents. Have a good evening, ma'am."

As the police car pulls away, the old man turns back to Gabby to yell, "Did you know that William Shatner is one of them? Turned 'Star Trek" into a Canuck propaganda show, too. Beware, lady. Beware!"

Chapter 47

The evening July sun is casting long shadows when Anna turns onto the Yellow Creek Nature Trail, running just far enough behind her to keep her in sight is Alys. Like Anna, Alys takes the right fork in the trail, knowing that the trail loops back around to eventually return to the fork. Unknown to both Anna and Gabby, Glenn entered the trail almost half an hour before Gabby and has taken up a concealed position from which he can clearly see the bench on which Gabby now awaits the rendezvous.

Anna comes running around the curve far to Gabby's left, her long strides slowing as she nears the designated bench. She stops, puts a foot up on the bench, as if to stretch her leg muscles while she glances back the way she came to see if anyone will come bounding around the curve. When no one appears, she sits down next to Anna, her breathing quickly returning to normal.

"Here's what I know. The file on the Marey photograph is missing from the museum's central files. One afternoon when I was the only one in the museum I went into Hudson's office but could not find it lying out. She has a couple locked file drawers, so it could be in there. Our computer catalog has few details about the work other than when we received it, who donated it, where it is stored when not on display, and such."

"So you hit a dead end?"

"With the original file I did. However, I remembered that when we had several volunteers working at entering our accession records into our database, we made photocopies of many of the records so that the workers could take them home to work on their own. We didn't have the money to purchase extra workstations just for the one time project of entering the records. So, anyway, I went to our long term storage area and found the box with the duplicate files. No one had bothered to toss them once the records were digitized."

"So you had some luck there?"

"A little. You already know who donated it and when. What was photocopied from the original file was the letter acknowledging the donation. However, what was odd about that was that Hudson, who signed the letter, put a value on the work. We do not do that as policy. Typically, there is an outside appraiser who provides an estimate of the value for tax purposes."

"We already knew that. The original copy of the letter was in the Stocker file, along with the Colonel's diary."

"But wait, there was a second page that had been copied and attached to the letter. It was a hand written note which read, 'copy attached to work'."

"What the heck does that mean?"

"I haven't a clue. We don't attach anything to works, as a rule. The photocopy of that note showed that its original had once been stapled to something. There were two holes in the upper left-hand corner where a staple had once been applied. But what was 'attached' I do not know. Could be that whoever photocopied the contents of that file forgot to copy that extra piece, or what it was attached to."

"Can you get me copies of those copies?"

"I'll have to wait for a time when Hudson is out. I did take the precaution of moving the copies to another file box, more or less misfiling it, so if someone comes looking for it, they won't be where they are supposed to be. But I was afraid to have the copies in my hand while walking around the museum. When I get the copies, I'll find a way to get them to you."

"You said you're being followed?"

"Ever since we had our drink that night I feel like someone is keeping track of my movements. That's why I haven't called and why I did not want you calling me at work. Here is my cell number and my personal email address." Anna then slips a business card from a side pocket of her running shorts and hands it to Gabby.

"Good thing we ran into each other at Farm and Fleet."

"That wasn't an accident. I was coming up West Street when I saw you turn into the Farm and Fleet parking lot, so I circled back around and came in after you. Ended up buying two packages of mouse traps I don't need just to make it look like I went in there on purpose."

Before Gabby could answer, there are sounds back up the trail from where the two are sitting and Irish Red begins barking. Anna immediately takes off in the original direction she'd been heading while Gabby and Irish Red start walking toward the sound of the noise. As they round the curve she sees Alys helping a man get back to his feet.

"I'm awfully sorry, sir. I didn't hear or see you and must have stepped into your path."

"Well, no harm done, I think."

As Gabby nears the two, a perplexed look on her face, she is startled by the sound of someone coming out of the undergrowth from behind her. She fails to notice Irish Red's wagging tale, a clear signal he knows the person causing the commotion. Turning to see the source of the noise Gabby is amazed to see Glenn.

"So much for leaving me alone to handle this. You two make a fine pair." Turning to the puzzled runner Alys accidentally on purpose tripped, Gabby continues, "I'm sorry, sir. My friend here was trying to play security and thought you're someone out to get me. I'm Gabriel Gordon and this is Alys Mendenhall."

"Oh, so you're Gabby Gordon. I'm Tim Rinker. I was the guy who chased off your attacker that night on Van Buren."

"Well, this is quite a coincidence. I've been meaning to call and thank you. Your timely arrival was very fortunate. And this guy, coming out of the woods like a later day Robin Hood, is Glenn Logan."

"Yes, thank you for coming to Gabby's aid," Glenn says as he shakes hands with Rinker. This moment of unplanned thanks is interrupted by the brief shrill of a police siren. Without comment or thought, all of them head for the beginning of the trail.

Rinker and Alys beat everyone there, but only by a couple seconds. The same Freeport Park District Police car is now blocking the south end of the bridge across Yellow Creek. As they round the squad car, they see the officer kneeling next to Anna, who is writhing in pain.

As Gabby reaches Anna, she kneels down and asks, "What the heck happened?"

"Some dirty, rotten, no good son-of-a-bitch ran up behind me and whacked me on the knee with a small ball bat. If I get my hands on that turd, I'm gonna use him as a scratching post for my cat."

"Did you get a look at him?" the officer asks.

"Yeah, he was wearing a stocking cap pulled down over the ears and then a Burberry plaid scarf tied over his mouth. He was wearing a light blue flannel jogging suit. Something out of the 1980s. Ahhhh, that really hurts."

"Officer?" Gabby queries.

"Ambulance is on the way. I'll radio the description to all the Freeport cars now on duty. Hopefully someone will spot the guy."

"You sure it was a guy?" Gabby asks of Anna.

"Yeah. The creep had hair on his forearms, I could see it because the sleeves were too short, as were the pants—high water. Besides, no woman would wear something that ugly and out of fashion. And to add insult to injury, that kid's ball bat he used has a Cardinal logo on it. Of all the nerve!"

When Gabby looks toward the policeman he is talking to a guy who arrived on the scene on a bicycle.

"Who's the dude in the form fitting cyclist's jersey?" Alys asks.

"He's the director of the Park District," Rinker remarks.

"Great set of abs. He must be into some heavy workouts for a man his age."

Tumbling Blocks

A small crowd has gathered near the end of the bridge by the time a Freeport Fire Department ambulance arrives.

"Miss Gordon, you seem to be at the scene of all the muggings these days," comments EMT Jay after they load Anna onto a gurney.

"Yeah, I'm starting to feel like a lightning rod for muggers."

Gabby takes Anna home from the hospital after the ER finishes with her, and the next afternoon Gabby goes to check on her at Anna's apartment. Hobbling with a brace on her leg, Anna is in pretty good spirits despite her injury.

"The orthopedist said the x-ray showed that I had a ligament sprain--a collateral sprain of the inside ligament."

"That doesn't sound good."

"Given the possible damage that could have been done, this is at the lower end of the scale. I'll have to wear this brace for up to six weeks, but probably less. But at least there is no permanent damage."

"That's good news, anyway. Can I get you anything? Groceries, a bottle of wine?"

"The wine sounds like a great idea, but not while I'm on pain killers. The only real drawback is that this'll kill my entry in the Chicago Marathon in October. I'll have to break my training schedule."

"I'm really sorry, Anna. Do you really believe that the attack was related to our meeting?"

"The odds seem to favor that. The police seem to think that the nature of the attack meant it was someone sending me a message."

"Maybe I've made it worse coming here."

"I'm not worried. The cops have been driving by every fifteen minutes or so."

"If you'd feel better, I'd be happy to have you come to stay out at my place. We have a Physician's Assistant on staff, plus an alarm system."

"Thanks, but I think I'll be OK here. As for your coming around, if they haven't figured out by now there's a connection between us, then they're dumber than we think."

"Well, if you're sure you feel safe here. I know it is more comforting to be in your own place, but I have lots of room, so you'd be no bother."

"I'll hang here. If things get hinkey, we can discuss the idea again. However, I'll need to stay home for a couple days, maybe a week. Anyway, that means it'll be awhile before I can get those copies for you."

"Don't worry about that. There's no reason to push yourself and maybe if we lay low for a while they'll be less likely to be watching."

"You could be right."

Chapter 48

S
am escorts Amery Stocker, Jr. into Gabby's office shortly
after 10:00 a.m., two days after the attack on Anna.

"Mr. Stocker, as promised, here are the contents of the
files in your father's name. The diary is there, as is the original
letter relating to the tax deduction for the donation to the
Freeport Art Museum."

"I appreciate your getting these to me. They are
meaningful to me and will be to my children someday, too. My
father was a hero, not only to his country but to his family and
to this town. I've never read his diary, so I am anxious to find
out the details of his exploits during the war."

"You should know that the Stephenson County Museum
made a copy of the diary, but I will turn it over to you unless
you are willing to give them permission to retain it."

"How did the museum get the diary?"

"I apologize for that. When we were sorting the files just
after the Bresch vault was opened, in a moment of excitement,
Dr. Barnes borrowed it without my knowledge. He did consult
with my secretary and left a note in the file about having it.
When I found out that he had it, I asked him to return it, but he
already had. Then he told me he had made a copy. I told him
that he had no right to do that without your permission. I have
the copy Barnes made here on my desk. If you want to take it
now you can and then decide later what you want done with it."

"Hmmmm. I am not happy that the copy was made
without my knowledge or consent," Stocker replies, though he
does not evidence any shock when told about Barnes' copying
the diary.

"I share your dismay over this. Believe me, had I known,
it would not have happened. I'm afraid that Dr. Barnes' zeal for
local history got the better of his professional judgment in this
case. I hope you can forgive him."

"I certainly have no ill will for Dr. Barnes. Perhaps I'll just take the copy for now. Once I've read the diary, I can consider whether or not to allow the museum to have it back."

"Thank you for being so considerate. Is there anything else we can do for you today?"

"No, Miss Gordon, you've been most helpful. Thank you for your assistance."

After Stocker leaves the building, Sam comes into Gabby's office closing the door behind her. "How did he take being told H had made a copy?" she asks.

"He showed no reaction and was perfectly calm."

"That's because he knew that a copy probably existed. I mean like he knew that Barnes had the diary at one time."

"You may be correct. He did not exhibit any emotion when I told him. Either he's a real cool one, or he really doesn't care."

"I wonder if you hadn't like told him if he would have asked?"

"We'll never know now."

"It's also curious that of all the calls and repeat calls about the Bresch files none came from Stocker."

Chapter 49

T he fact that Gabby and Sam have copied files they
figured might be the targets of whoever is attacking
people who had anything to do with the Bresch files is
kept a secret from the temp workers even after Gabby is
mugged. So, it is no surprise a few weeks after they were
installed by Alys that the surveillance cameras in The Raspitory
reveal someone tampering with the files.

"Can you explain why you were looking through the
files on Sam's desk?" Gabby demands quietly as she and Sam
have Anita Otway cornered by the back door of the office. At 5'
3", with a mousey complexion and straggly hair, her thick eye
glasses add to the image of someone who could easily be
intimidated by even a vociferous canary.

"I work here," is the weak response.

"But your duties do not call for you to look at files on
like my desk," Sam scowls as she puts her hands on her hips.

"I was checking to see if there were any more files with
the name 'Ossoli' on them before I began the next name in the
file box."

"Really? You think we'll buy that story? We have been
sorting files for weeks, and there are no more un-located files
which are in need of being reunited with files of the same
surname," Gabby says in almost a whisper.

The other three temporary workers are all staring at the
trio by the back door, not sure whether to intervene. Seeing the
attention they are getting, Gabby says aloud, "You guys can
head home for today. We're done. Thanks everyone. Have a
good evening. Oh, and remember that this Friday will be your
last day as our work here will soon be completed."

Not sure about abandoning their colleague, the three
slowly head for the other door, still watching the confrontation.
When the last one is out the door, Gabby pulls out her cell and
keys in a number on speed dial.

Tumbling Blocks

After a pause, Gabby says, "Detective Sumner, please." Another pause. "This is Gabby Gordon, we've caught someone trying to steal files from our office on Main Street. Can you please come over? Yes. And you probably ought to bring a couple uniformed officers to take her into custody. Thanks."

As she gets off the call, Gabby says to Anita, "The police will be here shortly. You want to cut a deal with us now or wait to see what the DA will offer?"

"Look, I...I...oh, hell. I knew I was gonna pay for this." With that she begins to sob, her hands instinctively covering her mouth to prevent anyone seeing it open so wide.

Gently, Gabby guides Anita to a chair and then sits down opposite her. Sam takes up a position standing behind Anita.

"You guys have been good to me 'cause I needed money and jobs are so hard to find. I know it was temporary work, but my husband has a shit load of traffic tickets cause he got nailed for DUI and then driving without a license. But he's got a good job and needs to get to work if we're gonna keep our house. So I was grateful when you hired me. But then this wo... person contacted me and offered me money to get some files, and sh...he... well, that person said that there was no danger. We really need the money for Jake's legal fees and I thought what could it hurt?"

"Who was the woman who hired you to get the file?" Gabby asks calmly.

"Don't know," Then Anita realizes that she has let the cat out of the bag. "How'd you know it's a woman?"

"Just a good guess, actually," Sam adds.

"But I don't know. She stopped me outside Aldi one day after I left work here; I had stopped there to pick-up some things for supper. Never said her name and I'd never seen her before."

"Can you describe her?"

"Well, short, kinda strange if you know what I mean."

"Strange how?"

156

"Wearin' a hoodie that was up over her head even though it was like ninety degrees. And she had on sunglasses. Real dark ones."

"How much did she offer you?"

"Five hundred dollars in cash."

"What files did she want?"

"There were three: David Knight, David Lathrop, and Amery Stocker, Senior."

"Did she say why she wanted them?"

"Said it would help keep someone out of trouble or something like that. How did you know that I was looking for files?"

"We have hidden video cameras that caught you," Gabby nods to Sam as she speaks. With that Sam goes over to the desk where Anita works and pulls out two files from a side drawer.

"Knight and Lathrop are here," she calls to Gabby from across the room.

"Couldn't find the Stocker file. Was going to look some more when everyone left tonight."

"Did this person give you a name?"

"No."

"How are you to let her know you have the files?"

"When I get all of them out of the building, I am to go to Krape Park and sit by the merry-go-round at seven at night until I was contacted, but I was not to bring the files with me. She had me give her my cell phone number."

"OK, Anita. Here's what you're going to do. Tonight go sit by the carousel at seven. When you get the call, we'll be watching and will follow you to wherever she tells you to go."

"What about the cops?"

"You don't worry about the cops. We won't tell them anything if you help us catch this mystery woman."

"But you called them."

"Actually, I called Sam's cell, which was on silent."

"Am I stupid or what?"

157

Anita sits by the Krape Park carousel from 6:45 till after 9:00 that night. All the while Alys is stationed west of the carousel on top of Flagstaff Hill with binoculars. Sam sits in Gabby's Ram Hemi pickup in the parking lot by the Yellow Creek spillway, a couple hundred yards to the northeast of the carousel. Gabby's behind the wheel. When no one calls Anita's cell, she leaves and her watchdogs quietly disappear.

The next morning Detective Sumner is waiting for Gabby at the Weston and Sanderson office when she arrives for work.

"Do you know an Anita Otway?" he questions once they are in her office with the door closed.

"Yes, she works for us organizing the files from the Bresch building. Why?"

"Her husband found her dead early this morning."

"What? Oh my goodness. Where? How?"

"In her car in the driveway of their home, over on Clark Street."

"He says she was out with you last night and never came home."

"Well, until nine. She went to Krape Park to see if the person who bribed her to steal files from me would contact her. Sitting by the Carousel was to be her signal to the contact when she had the files."

"Did you think you ought to have let us handle this?"

"Seemed harmless at the time."

"Three of you assaulted is not harmless, Miss Gordon. Now we've got a homicide on our hands."

"She was alone in her car when she left the park. I did not follow her home."

"Did she have the files with her?"

"No. We didn't let her take any and besides, her instructions from an anonymous caller were to not bring them to the park. Do you suppose the killer followed her from the park?"

Tumbling Blocks

"Good probability. How was she to contact the person seeking the files?"

"Anita had given the contact her cell number. We assumed that the contact would drive through the park, see her waiting, then call to setup a meeting. How did Anita die?"

"Strangled from behind using a scarf. One of the officers said it was a Berberet plaid."

"Burberry plaid?"

"Yeah, that's it."

"Didn't the guy who assaulted Anna Shaffer wear a Burberry plaid scarf?"

"You're right about that. How did Mrs. Otway get involved in stealing files?"

"Said she was stopped by a woman in the Aldi parking lot one day. The woman was wearing a hoodie and sunglasses, so Anita could not identify her, but she knew it was a woman."

"Why was Mrs. Otway helping this mystery woman?"

"Offered her $500 for three files, and her family finances are pretty bad right now."

"Which three files?"

"Knight, Lathrop and Stocker."

"Wasn't a Stocker file in the ones that Mrs. Bresch tried to take?"

"Yep. That's why we figured that the Knight and Lathrop files were red herrings."

"So, what's so important about the Stocker file?"

"We think it has to do with a diary that Colonel Stocker kept during World War II. It is supposed to be in the file."

"You think Amery has anything to do with all this?"

"I can't see why. He asked right after the vault was located that if his father's diary was in the files then he would like to have it. I gave it to him yesterday, but it would seem that someone else is very interested in it, too."

"You've read it?"

"No, Dr. Barnes did. Said it seems pretty bland, unless you're a World War II buff."

159

"Do you have a copy?"

"No, I gave the only copy to Stocker along with the original diary. Barnes had scanned the diary, without my knowledge, so I made him give me the digital file and his one hard copy. I gave both to Stocker along with the original copy of the diary."

"How did you know Otway was trying to steal files?"

"After the break in by Bresch, we had security cameras installed. We spotted Otway going through files on my secretary's desk when no one was around. When we confronted her, she quickly admitted her role and how she had been contacted."

"Well, we'll need you to stop over to the station to give a statement on what happened yesterday from your point of view. Were you the only one watching her last night?"

"No, Samantha Greer, my secretary was in my truck with me sitting by the spillway, and Alys Mendenhall was atop Flagstaff Hill. Anita was to sit on a bench near the Carousel until she was called. When no call came, we all left at about nine. I suppose all this will be in the news?"

"Well, we'll try to keep as many of the details away from the press as possible for now so we'll have leads to work on that the killer might not know we have. But if this comes to an arrest and trial, and there is a connection to the Bresch files, then, yes, it'll all come out."

After Sumner is gone, Gabby goes over to the Raspitory to inform Sam and the other workers about Anita's death. Shock and dismay are the general reactions. Gabby does not reveal to the temps about Anita being caught trying to steal files and the subsequent stakeout at Krape Park. But it is obvious to Sam later in the day that the other workers are worried that Anita's death had something to do with the confrontation the day before between Anita, Gabby and Sam. At quitting time all three workers inform Sam that they would not return to work the next day or ever.

Tumbling Blocks

By noon Gabby has given a formal statement to Sumner at the police station. Sam also volunteers her statement since she was involved in catching Anita and the subsequent planned trap. Alys is to go in the next morning.

Chapter 51

Gabby is very depressed when she arrives home that
evening. Glenn shows up unexpectedly and his buoyant
mood does not match hers at all. In fact, she is
downright irritated that he should be so upbeat, her mood
causing her not to ask the reason for his high spirits. After she
tells him about Anita's death, Glenn becomes subdued, taking
his glass of wine and plopping down on a chair out on the patio.

"I feel like I got that poor woman killed," Gabby laments
as she sits down next to Glenn. She then tells him about the plan
to find whoever had bribed Anita through the stakeout in Krape
Park.

"You couldn't have known that whoever is causing
problems would go to that extreme. Don't blame yourself for
this."

"How can I not take the blame? I talked her into being
the bait to catch a rat. Now that rat turned on her."

"I know it feels like you are responsible, but whoever
killed Otway is the killer. Who knows, maybe killing her after
she got the files was already planned. It is even possible that
whoever did this saw you talking to her in the office after work
and never even came to the park last night. If what you say is
true as to how quickly she caved into telling you the truth, it's
also possible the killer figured she would always be a liability
and planned to eliminate her as quickly as possible after the files
were delivered."

"I know logically all of that is possible, but it still
doesn't relieve the emotions of someone killed who you knew
and that their death is a result of some connection to what you're
trying to unravel."

They sit in silence for almost twenty minutes; both lost in their
own thoughts about the situation. A long period of silence ends
when something occurs to Gabby.

"Say, Double N, earlier you were pretty happy about something. I suspect that's why you showed up here when I didn't expect you. But I was so upset about Anita that I didn't give you a chance to tell me your news. So, what gives?"

"Got a letter from the Marriage Tribunal."

"Now what?" Gabby moans as she assumes more bad news coming.

"Oh, no. Not the Diocese of Madison Marriage Tribunal. This was from the Archdiocese of Washington, D.C. Marriage Tribunal."

"What do they have to do with anything?"

"To inform me that my marriage to Alexandra Paris has been annulled as directed by the 'See of Rome.' Yep, that's what it said, by the 'See of Rome,' whatever that is."

"What? How? Who? Rome?"

"We knew that Lexi is engaged to marry the son of a certain prominent United States Senator. It turns out when I ran an internet search I discovered that said senator and his family are very Catholic. So I think that Lexi, as the bride-to-be, needed her prior marriage to some obscure historical architect from Wisconsin annulled. She was granted an annulment 'in favor of faith' as the letter called it. I searched that phrase, too, and found that in the annulment field it is commonly used in the Petrine Privilege. Said annulments are only granted by the Pope."

"Did you know anything about her working on an annulment?"

"No. But, I recall getting a letter with one of those questionnaires at about the same time I completed an affidavit for my own annulment application. Irritated at being asked the same questions again, I simply copied the one I had already finished and mailed it back."

"Didn't that paperwork have the Madison Diocese letterhead?"

"I don't know. But all those names, diocese and archdiocese, and so forth, all get jumbled in my converted mind, so I figured what was good for one church bureaucrat was good for another church bureaucrat."

"And now you have an annulment thanks to the political connections of your ex-wife, while the annulment that rightfully belongs to you is lost in the bureaucracy due to some deacon's petty pique. Who says God doesn't have a sense of humor?"

"All that's left is for us to set a wedding date. Oh, and I do want to personally hand Deacon Herb a copy of the letter from Washington so I can see his reaction when he reads that the Pope has granted the annulment he himself tried to block. That will be rich."

"Sounds like I'll be going to Mass at Saint. Martha's with you this Sunday. I won't miss this for anything."
Before the weekend arrives, however, both Gabby and Glenn have second thoughts about confronting Deacon Herb. A photo copy of the letter from the Archdiocese of Washington announcing the annulment is simply forwarded to the pastor of Saint Martha and the matter is left at that.

Chapter 52

T he next day, Sam takes Gabby to lunch at 9 East Coffee just to get her out of the office and to try to get her mind off Anita's untimely death.

Sam tries to lighten Gabby's mood by telling her about one of Sam's misadventures with an injured baby opossum she adopted. While Gabby finds some humor in the epic tale of midnight feedings using a baby bottle and the hijinks that ensued as Sam drove all over northwest Illinois at three in the morning trying to find a veterinarian to treat the benighted critter, in the end it was mostly a futile endeavor.

As the two linger over their dessert lattes, Gabby begins talking about the news of Glenn's annulment. Again Sam professes a lack of understanding concerning the bureaucratic ways of the Catholic Church while she also shares Gabby's joy at finally being able to set a date for the wedding.

"Have you decided on the details?" Sam asks with her usual enthusiasm.

"We are going small, very small. Probably no more than ten guests for a quiet dinner at some local restaurant."

"What, no procession of bridesmaids and groomsmen?"

"No, not this time. Both of us just want a few close friends and immediate family."

"That may disappoint a host of people who would like to wish you well," Sam says softly as she stares into her cup.

Gabby realizes that Sam's now dour manner is a result of Sam thinking that with a very small wedding it is probable that Sam will not be invited. So, her mood having brightened with the infusion of the espresso in her latte, Gabby decides to have some fun with her secretary.

"I'm very set on having a bouzouki player at the wedding, but I know that Glenn wants to have an "NCIS" themed wedding. Can you see me dressed as Abby? And that for a wedding dress?"

Tumbling Blocks

"You've got to be kidding me!" Sam stammers. "Glenn really wants that type of wedding?"

"Well, we've not settled anything yet, but he thinks we ought to have everyone dress like a character from the TV show. I've never seen the show, so I guess I better watch it before I agree. But I'm holding out for the bouzouki and having someone to teach all of us Greek folk dances."

"Oh, Gabby, there has to be some reasonable middle ground with Glenn. He can't be serious. Maybe if you went for a 'Doctor Who' theme or even something from one of the Harry Potter books. But a TV crime drama. Really?"

At this point Sam finally looks Gabby full in the face to see her slight grin and the twinkle in her eyes.

"You dog. You've been putting me on."

"Sorry, Sam, but I could not resist pulling your chain a bit. We've really not discussed anything and with all the trouble with the Bresch files and falling buildings and now Anita's murder, I think we won't get around to making decisions for some time to come."

Chapter 53

Two evenings later, Gabby and Sam enter Walker Mortuary for the visitation for Anita. There are a few people there as Anita and her husband did not know many people in Freeport even though they both had lived there for over ten years.

As Gabby and Sam are leaving they run into Marissa Hillenbrand, one of the other temp workers at the Raspitory. Marissa is in her mid-thirties and works nights as a bartender at Harvey's Brew Pub and Grill. Though she has considerable secretarial skills, she prefers bartending, but took the temporary job at the Raspitory to save up money for a new car. Her bright red hair done in a punk rock spike makes her easy to spot in any crowd.

When Gabby sees that Marissa is alone, she approaches her with, "I'm sorry that you felt you had to quit so suddenly. I hope it wasn't something we did."
Looking around as if to determine who might be watching them, Marissa draws Gabby closer to say, "Did Anita's death have anything to do with files at work?"

"Why do you ask?"

"We-l-l-l, I saw you and Sam talking to her the afternoon before she was killed. She seemed really upset. Then I remembered that I was approached by a woman in a hoodie and sunglasses in the parking lot of Sullivan's a couple weeks back. She offered me three hundred bucks to steal some files from work. I told her to get lost. After you came to tell us that Anita had been killed the three of us started talking and that's when we figured out that we had all been approached in the same way. We were scared of working there anymore."

"I see. Do you think you could identify the woman?"

"I doubt it. She was wearing dark sweats. With the hood up I could not even see the color of her hair."

"How did you know it was a woman?"

Tumbling Blocks

"Her voice was a giveaway, along with the rattle of probably a bracelet. I did not see one, but I could hear jingling coming from somewhere."

"Marissa, you need to talk to Detective Sumner. Do you want me to have him call you?"

"No, I'll call to make an appointment tomorrow morning after Anita's funeral. I just feel awful about Anita. I hope my not telling you guys about that woman didn't put Anita in danger."

When Gabby gets back home after the visitation she finds Glenn waiting there. They snuggle together on a couch in the family room, the full reality of Anita's murder weighing heavily on Gabby's mind. At length, Glenn offers the suggestion that they get everyone together for a brain storming session to see where to go next or at least how to better protect themselves.

With Gabby's approval, Glenn sends a text message to Sam, Barnes, Alys, Sarah, and Anna asking them to come to Babcook Manor for dinner and a strategy session the next evening. Because her knee injury precludes Anna from driving Sam is to pick her up.

Chapter 54

T he last of the dinner dishes cleared away, the seven sit around the dining room table, the news of Anita's death still making the impromptu meal a very subdued affair. In spite of Glenn's pizza making skills, everyone seems deep in their own thoughts.

At last, Glenn breaks the silence. "It seems to me that the key to sorting all this out lies in figuring out what it is that someone wants to keep secret. If we can nail that down, then we will know where the attacks are coming from."

"Glenn is right on that. Let's run down a list of suspects to see what makes sense at this point," Gabby says, encouraged by an idea that at least points in a direction for some kind of action.

"I'll begin," Sam jumps in as a way of getting the ball rolling. "Bitter Betty wants the news about the off-shore accounts like kept silent."

"But she's in jail," Alys counters.

"Out on bail as of yesterday morning," Sam notes to everyone else's surprise.

"So, she has motive and opportunity, as the detectives say," Barnes muses.

"But the Bresch financial records were not among the files that Otway was supposed to steal," Sarah expands.

"True, and she is aware that we know about the off shore accounts and the impropriety with the Winfrey Estate, so she has nothing to gain by stealing some files," concludes Gabby. "Sarah, are you taking notes?"

"Kinda. I am a visual learner, so I think more clearly when I have facts written down." Sarah has her Day Runner open before her and is writing as the others talk.

"So, what about Stocker?" Alys asks by way of getting the discussion going again.

Tumbling Blocks

"He has the diary, so if there is anything in it that he wants kept secret, then it is already in his hands," Gabby mumbles as if she is actually thinking about something else.

"What was in that diary, anyway?" Glenn follows.

"Not much beyond the Colonel's movements during the war. Some detailed entries about how he was wounded in the Battle of the Hürtgen Forest and then his rehab in a hospital in England. There was a dalliance with a British nurse while recovering."

"Could Amery want to keep that secret? Was the Colonel married at the time?" Alys jumps in.

"Yes, he was married at the time and I was mildly surprised that he was so explicit with the details of the affair," Barnes responds. "But such affairs were common enough during the war, especially for officers. Eisenhower was rumored to have had an affair with a female who was his chauffer, I believe, and Patton bragged about having had an affair with his niece, a Red Cross volunteer."

"Besides, Mrs. Colonel Stocker is dead, so like who would Amery be protecting? Guys, it's like that kind of information is actually pretty much ignored these days," Sam snorts.

"Was there anything that happened when his troops occupied that town in Austria after the war? Sometimes they had trouble controlling the young American soldiers who had guns and nothing else to do," Alys speculates.

"He never mentioned anything specific about the occupation. I did discover while doing an Internet search the curious fact of the name of the village they occupied, 'Unken' means 'doom prophecy' in German. But I digress. All he wrote about, besides his desire to get home, was the beautiful house of a Nazi officer that he occupied while his unit was stationed in the town."

"Isn't that where he got the picture that was later donated to the Art Museum?" Anna asks, her question startling everyone as they had forgotten she is at the table since she had not spoken all evening.

"Yes, it was hanging in the house he occupied. He took it with him when he was sent home. According to the diary there were no living relatives of the family that originally owned the house, so he must have figured any of their belongings were fair game," Barnes concludes.

"Perhaps Amery is worried about a charge of thief against his sainted father," Alys notes.

"Considering that the theft took place over sixty-five years ago, that the Colonel is long dead and buried and that many Americans brought back such souvenirs, I doubt anyone would really care. Besides, the Colonel never made any secret about the fact that he brought it back with him," Barnes expands.

The group falls into silence for a couple minutes. Then Barnes renews the discussion.
"Now that I think about it, that's where the diary stops. There was at least one page torn out of the diary at the point where he had written that he was leaving the next day to begin the journey back to the US."

"So, is it possible that the picture is at the core of this?" Glenn poses.

"That kinda makes sense since the jewelry lady at the museum has been like playing games about that picture," Sam offers with a degree of venom that reveals her dislike for Hudson.

"Wait!" Gabby exclaims as she jumps out of her chair and points at Sarah. "What did you just fold and tuck into the pocket of your calendar book?"

"I wrote a note about groceries. Is there anything wrong with that?" Sarah offers in a slightly offended tone.
"Anna didn't you say that the file on the picture had a note in it that read, 'copy attached to work,' or something like that?"

"Yes, that's what was hand written on the back of the letter."

"Maybe that's where the missing page of the diary's hidden," Gabby says as she begins to pace the room. "Sarah folding a note and tucking it into a pocket of her calendar made me think of it."

"But we don't do things like that. The acid in the paper would be bad for the work of art in the long run," Anna explains.

"If Hudson has no idea it was there, then it could be there still, acid or no acid, right?" Glenn sums.

"I think that is where we need to go next. We've got to examine that picture. Anna, do you think it is in the museum somewhere?" asks Gabby.

"Could be. But it could take all of us searching for days to find it within the collection storage area if it is not in its proper place. Each work of art has a storage container or location where it is kept when not on display. We could look in the drawer where the picture is supposed to be kept. If it's not there, then I wouldn't know where to start looking."

"So, how do we proceed?" Alys asks enthusiastically.

"Can we gain access to the storage area tonight?" Gabby queries Anna.

"Well, yes. But we could just as well do it tomorrow," is Anna's hesitant response.

"But then we'd have Hudson there and she might try to stop us. I doubt we could get a search warrant based on our circumstantial evidence," Gabby admits.

"As an employee, you can grant us access to look at the picture, and that would best be done sans Hudson," Barnes intones.

"There is one potential problem," Anna adds. "When Sam stopped by to pick me up this evening, I did not know she was coming. She mentioned a text message, but I did not get it as my cell phone has been missing since I was attacked in the park."

"So," Sarah says as if thinking out loud, "it's possible that whoever attacked you took the phone and is aware of this little meeting. Maybe they're watching the house right now."

"Good point," Gabby walks into the living room to look out at River Road as she speaks. "There are no cars parked along the road, but since we've not been watching, someone could be driving by on a regular basis."

Back in the dining room, she continues, "Well, we need a plan that will throw off anyone who might be watching us."

"Look," Glenn suggests. "They can't watch all of us, because I don't think whoever this is has the manpower to do so. Principally, they will want to watch Gabby and Anna, since you two are the greatest potential threats. So, what we need to do is all go home and appear to go to bed for the evening. Act as if nothing is happening."

"Like lull them into a sense of like false security," Sam chimes in.

"Yeah. Then, at say two a.m., each of us will take up pre-determined spots around the Art Museum to watch. At two-thirty Gabby and Anna will arrive and they can go in to look for the picture. If any of us sees anyone following them or arriving at the museum, we can call Gabby's cell with the alert and then all of us will enter the museum like the cavalry arriving in the nick of time to save the wagon train."

"Sounds like a capitol plan," Barnes offers. "It could easily work. I can't imagine whoever is behind this will want to sit outside all night if they think we've all gone to bed."

"I don't like the idea of Anna or Sam or the good doctor going home alone tonight. Here in the Manor we've got strength in numbers as well as a security system," Gabby notes.

"Don't worry about me, my dear. With Alfred Thayer at my side, we'll prevail against any one bent on skullduggery," Barnes intones with a flourish.

"Will it like raise suspicions if Anna comes home with me?" Sam poses.

Tumbling Blocks

"It might. Anna's been living alone since she was attacked, so her suddenly spending the night at your place might tip them off," Glenn suggests.

"I've got it. I'll have to help Anna get into her apartment, so I can check the place to make sure no one is there. Then I'll head to my place. If like no one is following me, I'll circle back. There is a church parking lot behind the line of trees that like actually runs along the back edge of her apartment complex's parking lot. I'll park there and then come into Anna's apartment from the back side. We can like leave the same way at two."

"Sam, it sounds like you've done this before," Sarah quips.

"Yeah. I used to live in the same apartments and I had an affair with a married guy once and that's how he'd get to my place so his car wouldn't be seen in the apartment complex lot."

"Did the ruse work?"

"Like until the church had his car towed!"

Chapter 55

Anna punches in her PIN a second time and again the alarm system shows it as incorrect. "Damn," she mutters. "Hudson must have had my code deleted." Another attempt causes the system to register that it is "off" and that all doors and windows are closed—a green light replaces the blinking red one.

"So, your code is still in the system?" Gabby asks.

"No, I used the PIN of our receptionist. She once mentioned that she used her date of birth. Good thing I remembered that since there is only a ninety second delay between when the system detects an open door or window and the police are notified."

Using flashlights the two cross the reception room and then walk down a hall to a stairway that leads to the basement storage area of the former grade school.

"At least Hudson didn't have the locks rekeyed," Anna notes as she opens the deadbolt system to the artifact storage rooms.

Once the door to the storage area is open, Anna, her leg still in a brace, limps into the darkened room a couple paces before the sensor for the lights detect her movement and kick on the banks of UV blocked lights. To further cut down on UV rays the entire storage area has its outside windows blackened. In this instance, the blocked windows also prevent any neighbor from wondering why the lights in the museum are on at 2:45 AM.

"The Marey's permanent storage spot is in the set of steel drawers at the end of row nine," Anna says as they walk past dozens of sets of shelves and cabinets. They turn left down row nine and stop at the last set of drawers. Pulling out the next to the last drawer, both are relieved to see the picture lying on a bed of protective foam.

Pulling off a layer of paper-thin foam that covers the picture and its frame, Anna notes, "Now we'll see if anyone has removed whatever is supposed to be attached."

175

Tumbling Blocks

Taking the picture from its drawer, Anna carries it over to a waist high work table. She turns the picture face down and begins examining the back.

"This appears to be undisturbed since it was put in this frame. Well, maybe not. Look here, along this edge where the frame meets the picture's backing. There's a tight, unbroken abutment of the backing and frame all the way around, but for about eight inches here, where there is a slight gap, as if something is holding the backing away from the frame."

Reaching into a drawer on the work bench, Anna draws out long, needle nosed tweezers. Carefully inserting them into the gap, she begins to ease out a piece of folded paper.

"That looks like the same lined paper that's in the diary Stocker kept," Gabby whispers.

"It's been folded so that it fits within the width of the frame," Anna notes when she hands it to Gabby.

Unfolding the page, Gabby begins reading aloud: *December 5, 1945—On the train home! While waiting for our troop train at the station at Unken I was approached by an elderly Austrian who asked in broken English if I was the officer who was living in the house of Col. Hans Herrmann. He then told me that the Marey photograph in the house had once belonged to a local Jew, an accountant named Abraham Herschmann. When the village was cleansed of Jews, Herrmann stole the picture. I think the old coot thought his tale would cause me to take the picture back to the house. We won the war, so hell no!*

"That explains everything," Anna exhales in amazement. "This is stolen Jewish art!"

"Do you supposed Hudson knew that when the museum accepted it?"

"She's stupid, but not that stupid," responds Anna.

"You're damned right I ain't that stupid!"

Gabby and Anna, startled at the voice behind them, turn to see Hudson and Amery standing a few feet away. Amery is holding a pistol. Slowly Gabby pulls her cell phone out of her back jean pocket and hits a button.

"Turn it off and lay it down," Amery demands firmly.

Hitting another button, Gabby lays the phone on the work bench next to the Marey.

"There's no cell phone reception down here anyway," Hudson's slurred speech makes her difficult to understand. She's obviously been drinking.

"Don't move another muscle," Anna emphatically states after Gabby lays down the phone.

"Good advice," Amery seconds.

"You think I was going to turn down a chance for a Marey in our collection?" Hudson asks rhetorically. "For a museum this size to receive such a work of art, my job here would be secured forever."

"But didn't anyone question the donation at the time?" Anna puzzles.

"Oh, yeah. Doug Perkins, who was president of the museum board at the time. The dolt was going to ask that a background check be made on the history of the ownership of the print, but when Colonel Stocker found out Doug was having an affair with his secretary, we blackmailed him into silence."

"He's still on the board," Anna coughs incredulously.

"Oh, yes. He's my insurance policy. He won't let them get rid of me because I can tell too many tales; and I won't let him leave the board."

"All of this is ancient history," snorts Amery as he waves his pistol, which Gabby recognizes as a German Luger.

"Did your dad steal that from a Jew, too?" Gabby sneers as she nods toward the pistol.

"Actually, this is the pistol with which my father was shot during the battle in the Hürtgen Forest. Later he took it off the Nazi bastard after he killed him. Sort of a family trophy you might say. Now, enough of this chit-chat. Hand over the page from the diary."

Anna and Gabby look at each other. Neither move.

"Hand it over or I start capping knees."

"You're a real authority on knees," Anna hisses without moving.

"Only got yourself to blame. If you'd minded your own business and not gotten mixed up with this nosey lawyer and her meddling museum director pal, you'd be at home now all comfy and safe."

"I suppose you're the one who attacked Barnes and Sam?" Gabby queries.

"Old fool. Taking the diary out of the office was a mistake. Got what he deserved. Both of them. Too bad I couldn't find it in his office. Would've saved all of us a lot of trouble. By the way, where did he hide it?"

"He didn't. It was still inside the scanner on his desk," Gabby answers smugly.

"Huh! Serves me right for not being more computer savvy. Should have thought to look there. Oh, well."

"What are you going to do with us?"

"Two thieves caught breaking into the museum art collection. Had no choice but to shoot, since you were armed."

"We've got no guns," Anna retorts.

"You'll have them by the time the cops arrive."

"Amery, we can't have people shot in the museum. Think of the publicity," Hudson whines.

"I am. Be a big draw. People wanting to see where the two art thieves were gunned down by the museum director."

"What? I'm not going to shoot anyone!"

"Oh, don't worry, I'll do the shooting, but it'll look like you did it."

"But when the police ask me ..."

"You won't be able to answer," Gabby whispers. "He's going to shoot you with one of the guns he's going to plant on us, so it looks like you shot us in self-defense. Isn't that right?"

"That's your problem, missy; too smart for your own good. Too bad those mugs from Chicago didn't finish you off and that toady boyfriend of yours when they had the chance. If

Tumbling Blocks

Little Miss Wimp here had been a little more aggressive when she whacked you that night, we wouldn't be here now, either."

"I told you I hit her as hard as I could, for Pete's sake," Hudson cries. "You really gonna shoot me?"

"Relax, nothing's going to happen to you. Now, hand over that page."

At that instant the automated light switch, no longer sensing movement in the area, turns off the lights. Gabby feels someone push her behind the work counter and then out into the next aisle. "This way," Anna whispers as she grabs Gabby's arm and tugs her along in the darkness.

"Shit and shoved in it!" Gabby stammers as she trips along behind Anna. As they come around the end of a row of shelves, Gabby gasps when she sees a goat's head in the red glow of the emergency exit light.

"What the hell?"

"Too long of a story for now. Keep following me," Anna says under her breath.

As the two reach the doors to the storage room their movements turn the lights back on. Just as they open the door, a shot rings out and a bullet impacts the steel door, ricocheting off into the corridor.

The Parapet

When Gabby and Anna reach the bottom of the stairs, Anna announces in hushed, breathless tones, "You go on. I cannot hope to outrun them with the pain in my knee and this brace."

"I'm not going to leave you," Gabby exclaims as she tries to help Anna up onto the first steps.

"No, Gabby. Our only hope is for you to get help. They can't kill me until they're certain they have both of us and the paper. You getting away is my only hope. Now go!" With that Anna pushes Gabby toward the stairs and she backs into a darkened spandrel under the stairwell.

Once up the stairs from the basement, Gabby finds that Amery and Hudson have chained the back doors of the museum closed. Gabby has nowhere else to go but up. Racing up three flights of stairs to the third floor, she is more breathless than she figured she should have been when she reaches the top landing. Now she faces a door to the right and one to the left. Simply on impulse she tries the one on the left, but it is locked. Hearing footsteps below, she turns to the door on the right only to discover that it is some sort of storage closet, but at least it's open.

Finding a wall switch, Gabby flips it and the closet lights up with a blue fluorescent glow. Looking in desperation for a weapon or an escape, she sees a ladder that leads to a trap door in the ceiling.

With footsteps echoing off the walls of the stairwell Gabby begins to climb the ladder. Then she realizes she left the door open. Back on the floor, she pulls the door silently closed and turns the deadbolt.

Scampering up the ladder she is soon at the top, facing a hatch with a lever in the middle. Gabby struggles with the rusted metal of the hatch's opening mechanism. To herself Gabby half whispers, "Don't force it, get a bigger hammer' Dad always

180

says," so Gabby begins to jab at the lever with the heel of her free hand.

Two gunshots echo off the walls of the storage closet just as Gabby's shoulder's clear the hatch. Amery is trying to shoot out the deadbolt lock on the closet door. Two more shots follow as Gabby finally gets both feet onto the roof and stands erect. She slams the hatch closed, and then kicks at the lever hoping the repeated impacts might jam the mechanism.

Moving across the flat roof that covers what was once the gym of the old school, Gabby moves to the farthest corner from the hatch and leans against the two foot high wall of the parapet. *The tile roof over on the other part of the building is too steep and will probably be wet with dew,* she thinks to herself as she contemplates trying to jump across. So she starts yelling for help in the hope that Glenn, Sam or Barnes might hear her and then call the cops.

The yelling stops when she hears the crash of the hatch opening. Turning toward her only escape route, which is now blocked, she sees Amery's head and the Luger appear in the bluish moonlight, his face lit from below by the light in the closet. Soon both he and a wobbly Hudson are standing on the roof.

Advancing toward Gabby, Amery snarls, "You are more trouble than two year old twins on Mountain Dew. Where's the other one?"

Gabby shrugs and looks over the side.

"Now, unless you're also planning on jumping off the roof, too, which I would encourage, we've reached the end of this little farce. Hand over the paper, or I'll just take it off your dead body."

"Think, Amery, you can't shoot her up here. The whole fiction of art thieves won't make sense," Hudson pleads.

"Oh, shut-up you old cow. I'm tired of playing this game. I'm gonna end it here and now."

"Why are you worried about all this?" Gabby asks in an effort to stall for time. "The print was stolen over sixty years ago. The statute of limitations has run out on anything illegal about it."

"Matter of family pride. Don't want my father known as a looter of Jews, though God knows he had no use for the lot of them."

"Besides, there is no statute of limitations on the Nazi war crimes against the Jews," Hudson adds.

"As you lawyers would say, counselor, it's a moot point now. I've got the gun and all of this ends right here, right now. Hand over the page!"

With no options left, Gabby pulls the page from a pocket in her jeans and holds it out over the edge of the parapet preparing to drop it onto the lawn of the museum.

"You give me that, or ..." Amery steps forward as he levels the gun at Gabby's chest. Before he can pull the trigger, he jerks forward as something powerful hits his lower back. The pain of the impact drops him to his knees; the Luger falling beside him. In obvious agony he rolls over, his back arched as the pain of the impact causes him to cry out.

"And this is the statue of limitations running out on your sorry ass," sneers Glenn as he stands over Amery, a two foot tall marble sculpture of the Roman goddess Concordia in his hands. Still holding the sculpture like a ball bat, Glenn turns to Hudson and asks, "You got a taste for marble or are you gonna lay down your gun?"

"No gun," comes the swift reply as she holds her hands over her head. "But be careful with that. It's part of the Rawleigh collection."

Gabby quickly grabs the Luger, removes the clip and the round in the firing chamber before she lays it back on the roof. She then searches Amery and finds two more pistols, which she lays next to the Luger after she unloads them. As she steps back from the pile of handguns, voices from the direction of the hatch catch their attention.

Tumbling Blocks

"The cavalry has arrived," announces Sam as she turns toward the hatch. Two Freeport police officers, guns drawn, are already standing next to it.

"Officers, these people broke in here and attacked Mr. Stocker," shouts Hudson as she points to Gabby. "Arrest all of them. They were trying to steal that statue."

The two officers do not react to Hudson's rant as they wait for Detective Sumner to come up through the hatch.

"Do you know who I am? Hudson screams again and again.

Finally Gabby turns to the officers saying, "Would you get on your radio and see if anyone knows who this woman is? She obviously doesn't know."

From behind the officers, Detective Sumner steps saying, "Still going it alone, Miss Gordon? Good thing we've been watching your movements or we might not have been able to respond as quickly to the nine-one-one call from Mr. Logan. But now we'll have to sort out who is in the wrong here. As if all I need is more paperwork."

"I can help with that," Gabby says. "My cell phone is on a work bench in the basement, where it recorded a conversation between Stocker, Hudson, Anna and me. I think its contents will make your job a whole lot easier."

Walking over to Glenn as he sits the statue down on the roof, Gabby asks, "Where is Barnes?"

"He's downstairs with Anna. He did not want to leave her alone while the rest of us followed you up here. She's the one who opened the front door and then told us where you were headed."

"What about Alys and Sarah?"

"They're in their vehicles blocking in Amery and Hudson's cars in case they tried to evade capture."

"Seems like you've thought of everything," Gabby whispers as she hugs Glenn. Then she adds, "Nice job with the statue, Sir Galahad."

Tumbling Blocks

Glenn starts to say something when he is interrupted by an EMT named Jay who has just come up out of the hatchway. "Miss Gordon, I'm going to put you on my Christmas card list since you seem to be providing me job security." Then the EMT says into his radio, "Dispatch, respond the aerial ladder truck to my twenty. We've an injured man on a roof top. He can only be moved on a back board and the trap door to the roof is too narrow."

It is close to 5:30 a.m. when Gabby, Glenn, Anna and Sam emerge from the police station. Sunlight is beginning to brighten the horizon in the east as they head for their cars. Barnes, Alys and Sarah are waiting in the parking lot. Sam suggests they find some place for breakfast, so they head to Country Junction, one of Freeport's numerous "family restaurants."

Their food has just arrived when Glenn's cell phone startles them.

"It's Detective Sumner," Glenn says before he hits the talk button. "Hello, Detective. What's up? Really? Oh, that's tough. Well, we all figured it would be something like that. OK. Thanks for the update."

"Well, don't just sit there smiling, tell us what he said," Gabby demands in a mocking tone.

"While under the influence of pain killers in the ER, Amery admitted to killing Anita. Sumner figures that the confession won't hold up in court, but he's pretty sure that the DNA in some salvia they found on that Burberry scarf that Anita was choked with will be that of Amery, who wore the same scarf over his mouth when he attacked Anna. Plus the confession on your cell will clinch the deal."

"So they'll nail him on that charge, too. Good!" Anna chirps.

"Oh, and the ER doctors said that Amery has three broken vertebrae from his encounter with a certain priceless statue from the Rawleigh Collection. You suppose he'll sue me?"

184

"If he's that stupid, then I know a very good lawyer who will take the case *pro bono*."

"But what if I want someone besides Bono to represent me?"

"You know, you're a smart ass. I'm surprised you ever made it out of college. Did you mouth off to your profs like that?"

"No, I guess you just bring out the best in me."

Silence follows for a few seconds as Gabby and Glenn stare into each other's eyes before finally Sam jumps in to fill the awkward gap in conversation.

"So, what's everybody going to like do now…oops. Sorry, Gabby. Scratch the 'like.' So what's everybody going to do now that we won't have to play hide and seek with bad guys?"

"Personally, I'm going off to Chicago for a couple days to attend the annual dinner of the Caxton Club at the Newberry Library. It'll be a pleasant change of atmosphere to sit around listening to people brag about what rare books or manuscripts they've recently uncovered," Barnes says wistfully.

"H., you need me to look after Alfred Thayer while you're gone?" Sam asks.

"My dear, I am sure that Alfred Thayer will be delighted to have your companionship. And I think he has come to appreciate the 'Three Ks' you esteem so highly. Thank you. And, by-the-way, what do you have planned?"

"I've got enough comp time racked up from this whole thing that I'm gonna get together with a couple girlfriends from high school and we're gonna do a road trip to like Vegas."

"Sarah has a week's vacation coming, so I think we are going to motor up to Spooner. My family has a cabin up there on a secluded lake and we can spend the week fishing, watching bald eagles, and sitting around the camp fire," Alys notes wistfully.

"Don't let her fool any of you, especially if you think you might like to come along. There is no indoor plumbing, no shower and the outhouse this time of year is impossible to stomach. And, the nearest public restroom is five miles away at a truck stop," Sarah moans as she mocks Alys.

"What about you two?" Sam demands. "After all this you've got to do something different somewhere else."

"Actually, I've got my eye on this really neat southwestern style house near Krape Park that is in dire need of rehabbing," Gabby begins only to be cut off by Glenn.

"Wel-l-l-l-l," Glenn inserts as he smiles at Gabby. "No. OK, you tell."

"Let's just say we don't want any of you making any big plans for the fall. Babcook Manor will be hosting a wedding and your presence will be very welcome," is Gabby's response to Glenn's opening.

Epilogue

It is a crystal clear Saturday afternoon in early October with the temperature hovering around 70° when Gabby and Glenn emerge from the side chapel of St. Thomas Aquinas Church as husband and wife. Their parents witnessed the ceremony along with Barnes, attired in a kilt, serving as Best Man and Sam as Maid of Honor. Such is the extent of the guest list for the ceremony itself.

The reception at Babcook Manor includes 100 guests who wander around the vast lawn where blue and white striped tents cover a buffet line, a wine bar and a dance floor complete with DJ. Tables and chairs, also covered in blue and white cloth, dot the lawn. In honor of Irish Red's heritage, discrete signs are posted around the perimeter of the grounds of Babcook Manor proclaiming in Irish Gaelic: *"Faichill! Madra cac."* [Beware the dog crap!]

Finial

Tumbling Blocks

Caveats

While Étienne-Jules Marey (1830 – 1904) was a pioneer in photography, he did not create an image titled "Tumbling Blocks."

The fact that Main Street Bistro opened four months before the timeframe of this novel in the location herein described as "O'Maddy's" has been intentionally overlooked.

Tumbling Blocks

Acknowledgements

The following individuals provided invaluable assistance in the writing of this story:

- Megan Lopez for serving as the Grammar Police—a classic instance of the student becoming the teacher;
- John Gluscic, MD, and Shawn Shianna, MD, for input on medical terms and descriptions;
- Robert Plager, Esquire, and John Whiton, Esquire, who provided insights concerning the disposition of files from defunct law practices;
- The members of the Caxton Book Club: Jennifer Kanosky, Becky Connors, Teresa Julius, Mary Hartman and Shawn Shianna;
- Jayson DiModica, Freeport Fire Department;
- Jessica Modica, director of the Freeport Art Museum;
- James E. Finch for the cover photograph; and
- Cathy, my wife, who remains my first reader and best friend.

The reader should note, however, that any and all mistakes are mine and should not reflect on anyone identified above as having provided input.

Edward F. Finch
Freeport, Illinois

Previously Published by Edward F. Finch

Nonfiction
Beneath the Waves: The Life and Navy of CAPT. Edward L. Beach, Jr. Annapolis, MD: Naval Institute Press, 2010. [www.nip.org]

Fiction
Assassin Town: A Gabby Gordon Mystery, Winchilsea Press, 2015. [www.Amazon.com]

Join the discussion about Gabby Gordon on Facebook.

Follow the author at www.edwardfinch.net

NB: Winchilsea Press neither solicits nor accepts manuscripts or submission queries.

59710994R00108

Made in the USA
Lexington, KY
17 January 2017